Advance Praise

"Marina Antropow Cramer's *Marfa's River*, is a quiet, moving, beautifully told story about a woman forced by famine and war to immigrate to a new country, away from all that she's ever known. She has endured the unspeakable and survived, while knowing that the spark of life in her is nearly extinguished. This is a story, not of battlefields, but of the steady endurance and dignity necessary to reclaim a life. It happens without fanfare, silently, through the kindness of others and through her openness to the small beauties of the world: a simple room filled with the aroma of a spicy ragout, a stray beam of setting sunlight, a black velvet hat with a curved green feather."

> — Eleanor Morse, author of *Margreete's Harbor* and *White Dog Fell from the Sky*

"Set in 1956 Brussels, *Marfa's River* is a beautifully wrought, luminous portrait of a woman trying to find her place in a troubled world. Marfa is a noticer. She listens carefully to the people around her. She observes the smallest shimmer in a person's eyes, as well as the things that people fail to say. She is willing and brave, despite evidence that for her, hope is a luxury.

Marfa is like a river, flowing and bending to fit in wherever she is able. Reserved though she is, her mind is full of keen observations, which Cramer allows readers to access in intermittent first person, stream-of-consciousness sections.

Cramer's writing is understated, precise, and elegant, and paints a portrait of the way we obscure our pain in order to survive our broken hearts."

— N. West Moss is the author of *The Subway Stops at Bryant Park* and *Flesh & Blood: Reflections on Infertility, Family, and Creating a Bountiful Life*

"In *Marfa's River*, Marina Antropow Cramer, a modern Russian refugee who settled in America, is presenting Marfa, a Ukrainian refugee of the nineteen-fifties, who settled in Belgium right after WWII. With a deft hand, Marina paints a compelling picture of a familiar yet fresh story of a war victim abused by both the Nazis and the Soviets. Marina is simply a master of words. Marry that with the compelling plot and international characters, and you get a winner."

— Mark Budman is the author of the story collections *Accidental American Odyssey* and *The Most Excellent Immigrant*, and editor (with Susan O'Neill), of the anthology *Short Vigorous Roots*.

"To read *Marfa's River* is to enter the soul of Marfa, a refugee from Ukraine in post WWII Belgium. Cramer's is the language of a looking glass through which to witness the genuine consciousness of a woman caught between the longings and regrets of her past and a fragile uncertain hope inside her present. An undulating tide of emotions flows through *Marfa's River*. Cramer gives us a story and a character that can't help but enter our hearts."

— Nancy Burke, author of *Only the Women are Burning, If I Could Paint the Moon Black* and *From the Abuelas' Window*

MARFA'S RIVER

Marina Antropow Cramer

Apprentice
House Press
Loyola University Maryland

This is a work of fiction. Names, characters, businesses, places, events, locations and incidents are either the products of the author's imagination or used in a fictitious manner. Any resemblance to actual persons, living or deceased, or actual events is purely coincidental.

"Let's Read," appeared in the Summer 2021 issue of *the other side of hope* literary journal in slightly different form.

First Edition

Library of Congress Control Number: 2022949979

Hardcover ISBN: 978-1-62720-431-6
Paperback ISBN: 978-1-62720-432-3
Ebook ISBN: 978-1-62720-433-0

Design by Brian Leechow
Cover art by Bo G Eriksson
Editorial Development by Carlos Balazs
Promotional Development by Corrine Moulds

Published by Apprentice House Press

Apprentice
House Press
Loyola University Maryland

Loyola University Maryland
4501 N. Charles Street, Baltimore, MD 21210
410.617.5265
www.ApprenticeHouse.com
info@ApprenticeHouse.com

Woman, you spread yourself in secret, like a shawl,
In a shawl, like a secret, you linger
Set apart—like a single surviving
Spruce on a misted summit.
—*Marina Tsvetaeva, "Under a Shawl"*
  Mary Jane White, translator, After Russia (Adelaide Books)

This thing you call heart can't be tidied like a purse
The mind can't be rearranged like a room
That's why I will say
just help me
don't ask why
—*Karin Karakasli, "Succour"*
  Canan Marasligil, translator (with Sarah Howe)

To Frank

Tolik, child of my enemy.

If you had looked like me, if you had taken my long face, my scowling mouth, the deep lines etched into my chin at birth in an expression the world would read as disapproval, maybe then I might never have loved you. If you had looked at me with eyes the color of mud, set too close to an upturned nose. If your hair had sprung like wire in rusty tufts around your head, behind large ears so undeniably mine, I could have pitied you, knowing the misery life had prepared for you.

But you were perfect. Silky, angelic. Your long slim fingers nothing like the stubby ones on hands too wide for my thin wrists. Fingers made for turning the pages of a book or strumming a balalaika, not shoveling dung, milking the cow, beating laundry. Fine hands of the oppressor I tolerated who touched my cheek and called me lovely. Me, Marfa.

No, I did not believe him! But also, I did. I let my knees fold, welcomed his mouth on my neck in spite of myself. I did. What choice did I have?

And after he was gone, Tolik, you came. And I loved you.

PART 1

1

Brussels, 1956

Marfa can hear shouting as soon as she enters the stairwell at 17 Rue de la Querelle. The house is old, its faded brick façade powdered with mortar dust. "The one with the green window frames, there," the woman at the corner store had directed, taking a ruddy hand out of the pocket of her smock to gesture down the rain-washed street. "Tell them to put a number on it and finish painting the trim." Marfa hears her mutter, "Immigrants," before she shuts the door.

The first floor windows are tall, one freshly outlined in dark green paint, the other one peeling, the sill repaired with a strip of raw wood that stands out like a scar on a wounded soldier. Marfa shakes the thought away. It's just a piece of wood, she tells herself. The war's over.

The narrow stairs are unpainted but swept clean. The man's angry voice carries a whining note that reminds her of her father. Only Tato didn't shout; his rage came in whispers, disguised as ordinary speech.

On the third floor, the door stands open.

"Why are you here?"

Marfa starts to reply, but the man's back is turned. She can't see who he's talking to.

"Did I raise a son to be a delivery boy? Why do you think I run this studio if not for your benefit, your future?"

Marfa edges along the wall of the room, under a slanted

ceiling held up at intervals by seasoned roof beams. She thinks of leaving. The unfolding family drama makes her feel like an intruder, even though none of the people seated at long tables along the windows raise their heads from their work. Charles Aznavour croons a love song from a station tuned to Radio Luxembourg, his gravelly tenor an odd counterpoint to the confrontation in the room.

No, she decides. It's already late afternoon. After weeks of facing closed doors and regretful head-shaking, she's not leaving without making an effort. She's hungry. She waits.

The boy stands, shoulders stooped, his jaw set in a hard line as if he's fighting back a reply. He is slightly plump, a full head shorter than his brawny father. "The Belgians will give you schooling," the man continues. "You can study law, engineering, anything. You think I wanted to be a rug dealer? If only I'd had your opportunities, if there had been no war. What future is there in doodling with paints and notebooks?" He waves his arm in the air. Marfa sees the boy cringe and step back. "Say something! Be a man for once." The man drops his arm to his side, takes a cigarette from a box on the sill, lights it and inhales.

The boy pushes a lock of hair off his forehead. "You smoke too much." He starts toward the door.

"Where are you going?"

"To finish the window, outside."

"At least that's useful. Get the damn city beautification people off my back. Goddamn socialists," the man grumbles, then shouts at his son's retreating back, "But I could have a workman do it."

Marfa moves aside to let the boy pass. He's older than she had first thought, but surely not more than nineteen, the age she had been when Hitler was defeated eleven years ago. His face is flushed, there's a hint of a tremor around his mouth and chin. His gray-green eyes lock with her brown ones for a moment; they flash with rage and frustration.

"Why are you here?" It takes her a moment to realize the man is now addressing her.

"I... the work," she stammers. "My friends Galina and Filip, they said you have work."

"So they're gone, are they? To America." He sighs. "That's where the future is. He had a good hand, Filip, a nice touch on the canvas. And Galina, a hard worker. What can you do?" His eyes are the color of seawater, the same as his son's but piercing, impatient. "Speak up. I can't stand here talking all day."

"I can clean, cook —"

"We don't need servants here. Can you paint, from a pattern?"

Marfa raises her chin, determined not to walk away with nothing. "I can learn," she says. "Teach me."

2

The man, Mehmet—everyone calls him Meti, or *Patron*—has her sit at the end of the last table, next to a blonde woman whose waved hair reminds her of England's new Queen Elizabeth. "Chantal will show you what to do. Pay attention." He lights another cigarette and stands looking down at the street, blowing smoke out the open window.

The room is warm. Marfa imagines it will be uncomfortable in the coming summer, wonders if there will be fans to dispel the paint fumes and the underlying tang of cotton canvas and glue. Now, the early evening breeze still carries a chill, a reminder of a season so severe, the newspapers had claimed Winter 1955 was one for the history record books.

"Does he always yell so much?" Marfa whispers when Meti has retreated to his desk in the far corner. He picks up some papers, holds them in his hand without looking at them. After a moment, he lets them drift back onto the pile on the desk.

Chantal shoots her a sideways glance. "You get used to it. Here, you see this flower? Watch." She points to a section of the floral pattern propped up on a table easel in front of her canvas. "Count the squares and fill it in." She dips her brush in yellow. The rose blooms under her hand.

Marfa is enchanted, eager to try. She takes the brush from Chantal, hesitates. "What if I make a mistake?"

"You can paint over it. Just make sure you see it before

he does. Now hush."

They work in silence because Meti demands it. "Too much talk means too many mistakes, and mistakes cost money. So no chatter," he tells Marfa.

"He doesn't know a woman can cook a meal with a child on her hip and another at her skirt, talking all the while and thinking about how to stretch the money until next pay day," Chantal retorts. "It's men who can do only one thing at a time."

Marfa thinks it bold. She catches her breath, expecting another blowup, but Meti just glares at the woman and grumbles, "Get to work."

"I never stopped, if you noticed," she answers, her voice lowered. If Chantal enjoys special status here she knows her limits, too.

The tables are covered with brown butcher paper stippled red, yellow, green, where the paint drips through the canvas holes. All but two of the workers are women. Glancing down the two long tables, Marfa counts eleven people, each bent over the work. The only sound in the room is Meti shuffling papers on his desk, and the radio, where Edith Piaf lays her heart bare, regretting nothing. *Rien de rien.*

Most of the women wear kerchiefs over their hair, tied at the nape of the neck; three wear the Muslim scarf. Some have high cheekbones and that cautious look she recognizes as distinctly Slavic. She's not sure she's pleased about the prospect of talking with them in her own language, if lapsing into Russian or Ukrainian might lead to revelations about the past she would prefer to keep to herself. The two men are in round cloth caps—the kind she has seen on fruit vendors at the weekly bazaar. The rest appear to be European, Belgians, she guesses from the confident way they hold their bodies, one leg crossed over the other. At home.

When daylight begins to fade, Meti turns on a string of bare bulbs along the window above the work tables. Several people shift position to avoid working in their own shadow.

"Serge," Chantal calls out when the boy re-enters the room. "Give me a fresh piece. She —" she tips her head in Marfa's direction, "— she can finish this one."

Serge places the blank canvas next to Marfa's nearly completed one. "Use the same design," he tells Chantal. "We can always sell more roses." Chantal pencils her initials on the bottom edge, turns the canvas over and starts filling in foliage in the upper left corner. She paints rapidly, as if from memory, humming a little tune Marfa recognizes as an advertising ditty for face cream.

Serge stands behind Marfa's shoulder, watching her move the brush with painstaking care. Marfa flushes red but keeps working, raising her eyes only to study the pattern she is copying. "Look, here." He leans forward and points at the rose she has just finished. Marfa catches a whiff of cologne, a hint of hair oil; the aroma is pleasing, masculine and boyish. "It's darker in the center, where the petals meet. Give me the brush."

He spreads a dab of yellow paint on the edge of the butcher paper, adds a single drop of red and stirs it around to make a deeper shade, a kind of pale orange tinged with pink. "Use this for the heart." The rose comes alive, taking on depth under her careful strokes. She looks up at him, delighted.

"Good," Serge says. His eyes look soft, but he does not return her smile. "You'll have to work faster, though."

Meti, his shirt sleeves rolled up to the elbows, is reading the newspaper at his desk. Serge flips through some finished canvases stacked on a cabinet near the door, slips a dozen or so into a leather portfolio. "I'll take these to Grand' Place in the morning, to the needlework shop," he tells his father, and leaves. Meti acknowledges with a wave of his hand. The tension in the room is gone; Marfa suspects the scene she witnessed is a regular occurrence, part of the push-pull of their family reality.

At 6:55, the alarm clock on Meti's desk clangs. All work stops. Chantal covers the paint pots, shows Marfa how to clean the brushes. Everyone files out, carrying small baskets or dinner pails, talking, laughing.

Marfa stops at the desk, not sure what is expected of her. Meti puts down his newspaper. "We paint Monday through Thursday. I pay on Thursday evening. It's piece-work, so you'll have to pick up the pace if you want to earn any money. The one you finished goes to Chantal, for training you."

It's only Tuesday. She nods and tightens her muscles, hoping he can't hear her stomach rumbling. But of course he does.

"You people," he sighs. He gives her a little money. "Be here at seven. Don't be late."

3

I took the money. Hadn't I worked for it? My hand held the brush that finished that canvas, even if someone else could have done it faster or better. Take what is offered: every refugee knows this. If there is to be a price for his generosity... well, I'm not as green as I look.

We survivors, we all have stories. The details may be different but the essence is the same. What protects women against the urgent needs of men? Whether they take us by pleading or by force makes little difference. Those who have not suffered judge us; they underestimate the value of a clean bed, food without worms or mold, a child to love.

Pride is a luxury only martyrs can afford. They hold to their principles and starve, secure in their moral superiority while I take my place among the fallen, moving from day to day in what passes for life. Which is better? I don't know.

Their broad faces tell me some of the women are likely to be from Russia. The middle-aged one with the haunted look is positively Ukrainian. She wears her hair parted in the middle and pulled into a tight bun, just like Auntie Safronia did. When she walked past me, her basket smelled of the dark homemade bread she brings for her dinner, heavy and yeasty like the loaves we baked in the backyard oven once a week, back in the good times. Before the hunger. Times we didn't know were good until they were over and there was nothing to eat. The grain collectors, evil as the devil himself, emptied our storehouses and cellars and took our livestock. Six years old, but I remember them carrying off our piglet, our goat, our chickens.

1932. Holodomor. The word chills me now just as it did more than twenty years ago. People said, how dreadful it must be for our country if even here, with the richest black soil on earth, there is nothing to eat. We thought everyone suffered like us. When there was time for thinking; when we weren't burying our babies in little pine coffins, two or three to a grave.

In the Nazi labor camp, I asked Galina if she remembered the famine. "Famine?" she said. "No. In the 30s? Not in Yalta. We lived on rations, but we didn't starve. What I remember is Red Army officers and their families strolling the avenues, swimming in the Black Sea. Anyway, I was small. My parents protected me." I was small, too. But hunger—the kind that consumes your brain like fire, twisting your guts into knots that crying only makes tighter—that is not easily forgotten. When people look at you with the eyes of a corpse, understanding nothing, and children suck their sleeves in desperation. Forget?

With Meti's money, I can buy bread and milk. My room is paid until the end of the week. I'll walk home tonight to save a few coins for trolley fare tomorrow.

What to make of Meti? Is his anger born of disappointment—in his life, his son, his business? He's younger than my father would be, by ten years or so. But I sense decency in him, good will. Tato had no use for good will.

4

Marfa likes the work well enough, the hypnotic rhythm of it. Once she comes to know the patterns and settles into the routine: dip, count, paint, dip—she lets her thoughts wander. Did the others do the same? What did they think about, families, children? After several weeks of twelve-hour days in the same room, she still knows nothing of their lives.

On fine days they eat their dinner around the corner, in the Place du Jeu de Balle. Marfa quickly learns which women always share a bench, which ones leave themselves a few minutes every day to dip their fingers in the holy water font or light a candle inside Notre-Dame Immaculée, the church that faces one side of the cobblestone square. The two men in cloth caps keep to themselves, talking together and smoking. They can't be more than twenty, Marfa guesses; maybe the mundane conversation of women bores them.

From time to time everyone strolls among the flea market vendors who occupy the square, perusing the shabby wares spread out on rugs and blankets on the ground: ten years since the end of the war, people are rich in chipped china, mismatched silver, mounds of old clothing, and broken toys. Marfa looks but does not touch.

This day, the day of the bee, Marfa crouches at the curb outside the church, eating her kasha and fried onions. There is room at the end of one of the benches, but she doesn't dare approach the Belgian women from the studio. She finds them brash, intimidating. In the time she's been working with them, not one has mumbled more than a curt *hello* or *good night*. It's just as well; she can't imagine what she would say to them. The presence of the immigrant women is more comforting, but they, too, have kept their distance.

Her meal finished, she contemplates the earthen flower tubs on either side of the church doors, their blooms in vibrant relief against the weathered stone walls. Real flowers, geraniums and lilies and purple daisies and others she cannot name. They bow to the breeze, turn their faces toward the sun, their leaves every shade of green. Insects go about their urgent business: a pale, nearly transparent caterpillar measures the length of a leaf, its outsized black bead eyes flashing a warning; ants labor up smooth stems and down again; a brilliant blue butterfly rests on a blossom and is gone. A bee skips and hums, skips and hums.

In the studio, work resumes. While they were out, Serge opened all the windows, the casements flung wide to let in the spring air. He sits in his father's chair, watching everyone file in. Meti is out.

Marfa paints. She has done this same design at least six times in the last two weeks. It goes faster, but she's beginning to chafe at the repetition. "Oh," she says, when a dot of yellow drips from her brush and lands on a dusky pink rose. "No." She could scrape the error away, but the pink is not quite dry and will smear.

Meti comes in and leans a roll of butcher paper against the wall. "Oof," he pants. "Next time you go, Serge. I'm too old to lug fifty kilos up those stairs."

"You're fifty-two. That's not old. But you could have a workman do it," Serge reminds him without looking up from the notebook open on the desk in front of him.

"Why pay a workman when I have a son? My son the poet. Get up, I need to sit down."

"What's this, then?" Serge picks up a small book, the cover decorated with red and orange scroll designs. He opens it, turns some pages. "Looks like poetry to me."

"That's literature, not schoolboy scribbling. Put it down," Meti says. "You can't read Turkish."

Marfa is too engrossed in worrying about her error to pay much attention to the brewing argument. She stares at the little blob, now nearly dry in the warm air wafting across the canvas. On a whim, she picks up the finest brush, dips it in black, and strokes in two stripes and the suggestion of a wing.

"What are you doing?" Chantal whispers, loud enough for all to hear. "Have you lost your mind?"

All work stops. Meti and Serge stand over Marfa. "What's this?" Meti demands.

"A.... a bee?" Marfa shrinks against her seat as if she would disappear into its worn wooden back.

"What the hell? What bee? Do you see a damn bee here?" He shakes an accusing finger at the pattern.

"I... I..."

"I like the bee," Serge says behind her other shoulder. "I think we could sell it."

The quarrel bounces from left to right and back again over Marfa's head, like an angel/devil contest, each using its powers of persuasion to win the battle of good versus evil. She might almost laugh if she weren't paralyzed with fear.

"Sell it? Sell it? We sell floral rug designs, not goddamn landscapes."

"It's a sweet touch. People will like it, I guarantee."

"*You* gua-ran-tee?" Meti stretches the word out, laying mockery on top of sarcasm. "She ruins the canvas and you *gua-ran-tee* her stupidity is an improvement?"

"I'll show it as a prototype. You'll see." Serge taps Marfa's arm. "Let me know when you've finished the rest of the design. And leave the bee alone."

By the end of the week, Serge comes in and tosses a sheaf of orders on Meti's desk. "Every shop will take at least one," Serge says, quietly triumphant. "Though a few would prefer a butterfly."

"We don't take special orders." Meti pushes the papers around with one hand.

"We do now. Besides, where's your pride in your Ottoman sultan heritage? Weren't their paintings full of animals and birds? I'm sure you'll find butterflies and bees, too, if you look closely."

"I'm no sultan. My father sold pomegranates in the street. He didn't ask his customers if they would prefer figs." He draws on his cigarette and peers at his son through the smoke. "We'll see how many of your insects come back unsold."

Serge ignores the remark. He addresses the two men and several women, including Marfa. "Here are the new designs. Finish the one you're doing and get to work on these."

In the end, a handful of the new canvases are returned, but only because, in the words of one merchant, some craft enthusiasts are not skilled enough to render small details. "They are accustomed to hooking their rugs in wool," he explains. "They don't know how to use silk to add the finer touches."

Meti looks smug until Serge adds, "You know what they want? Smaller, square canvases, suitable for a wall picture or pillow cover, with no flowers, only a single bee or dragonfly. Think of the color possibilities of a butterfly, on neutral ground. Or black! Can't you see it, Papa?" He starts sketching on the back of the nearest invoice. He raises his pencil and waves his hand around the room. "These simple designs are fast and easy to paint. Our people will enjoy working on them. And they will sell."

"Figs," Meti says. "We offer pomegranates and they want figs." He looks deflated. "Do what you want. I'm going to the baths."

5

Meti could have fired me for the stupid bee. I wish he had.

What possessed me? It's not as if I'm any kind of artist. If Chantal hadn't noticed, I would have painted over the dumb thing and no one would have known it was ever there.

It must have been the flowers. The real ones, outside the church, not these flat imitations. The ones that dust your fingers with pollen, their aroma carried on the breeze. And insects, the humble and the beautiful. What are flowers without insects—bees and wasps and butterflies—to do the work that keeps them blooming from one year to the next?

That's the way it is. Someone has to do the work, so thinkers can think and planners can plan. Someone has to sweep and cook and fix things, to keep the shine on the glass and the grime out of the corners.

I've always been the worker ant alongside others in the village, doing what I'm told or anticipating Tato's demands so he wouldn't speak to me in that icy way, making me feel stupid, slow. Unless he'd been drinking. But that's another matter. Toiling with the women was satisfying, even if I was still a girl, eager to leave school behind and run off to the fields. No one had to tell me I was a good worker; it didn't matter whose hand harvested which stalk of wheat for the collective benefit. When our production was not enough to fill the people's needs we all suffered, not just me.

Listen to me. When did I get so philosophical?

When Meti and Serge started arguing about the bee, I could feel all eyes on me, accusing, angry. Who did I think I was, coming into their ordered world, disturbing the work they all depend on, stirring up trouble? I hate being the center of attention. I wanted to run and hide, pretend it never happened, return to my place in line and paint flowers, obediently, like everyone else. I had begun to hope that among the people in that room I might find, if not friendship, at least, eventually, some warmth. Now I'm not so sure.

Does being alone ever stop weighing down your soul?

But Serge would not let it be. Now there's resentment and discord, and it's all my fault.

Butterflies on black ground. Like Tolik's tiny hand against the black water. I shuddered, my head full of the rush of the infernal swollen river. It all got muddled after Serge's fingers brushed my arm and sent a shock through my body. Why did I feel so dizzy and confused? Then I was dancing with Petro at the village May Day feast, his hand on my hip, both of us laughing until we weren't.

So what if every picture is the same, even if the colors are different? So what if every canvas is as dead as all others? Dead. Like Tato and Auntie Safronia. Tolik. And Petro, too, who will never fix another tractor, will never again smile at me with his eyes. And ... and ...

6

The bee turns out not to be the most popular of the new designs. Butterflies quickly take the lead, followed by a handsome dragonfly.

"They like the smaller canvases," Serge tells his father. "Striking, and easy enough for children to do."

Meti grunts. "Until they get tired of bugs and want something new. Then what? Cats and dogs? The Taj Mahal?" He snorts and walks away, stands at the window, smoking. "Flowers are universal. Nobody gets tired of flowers."

"I was thinking maybe birds," Serge says seriously. "But you're right about flowers. Look at these." He spreads some sketches on the desk and steps back.

Meti stubs his cigarette out on the windowsill and flicks the butt out the window.

"Don't let *Maman* see you do that," Serge says. "She'd make me go out and pick it up, and sweep the sidewalk, too."

Meti throws him a cold look. He saunters over to the desk. "The chrysanthemum, yes, and the tulip, though I would do a pair, with foliage. The rosebud is too sentimental." He speaks in a monotone, as if grudging the words.

"Not sentimental, Papa. Romantic. Haven't you noticed?" He gestures at the radio. "Nothing but love songs all day long."

"Young people think they invented love. In the war —"

"Who wants to hear about the war? People want to live. People want romance."

"How do you know, at your age, what people want?"

"I don't spend my time in a Turkish café reading week-old newspapers from home and reminiscing about the past with men from the old country."

Meti turns pale. "What gives you the right to talk to me like that? To tell me how to live? I'm your father and you're... you're..." he sputters, his face red, and strides out of the studio.

"Serge?" One of the men in cloth caps looks up. "Some of us are finished. Do we make more butterflies?"

"What? Yes, all right." Serge hands out blank canvas squares and picks up painted ones. "You do blue, and you, orange." He turns to Marfa. "What are you working on?"

"A bee."

"When you're done, start on this one."

He steps out into the hall, leaving the door open. Meti stands with his back against the wall; his breathing is raspy, his fingers twitch.

"Papa," Serge says. "Calm down. I meant no disrespect. People want something new, and not just in needlework. I read magazines, I talk to students and shop customers. Even *Maman's* friends are trying new foods, reading books full of new ideas. The world is changing. Has changed. Calm down," he repeats. "This agitation is bad for your heart." He lays a hand on Meti's shoulder.

Meti shrugs it off. "You should have thought of that before you opened your mouth," he huffs. "Time for the dinner break."

Marfa starts to go out with the others. She can smell

the garlic in her vegetable stew through the closed lid of her dinner pail; the thought of eating it out in the hot sun makes her nauseous. Voices from the square float on the stifling air—buyers and sellers, an argument, a police whistle. Dogs and babies. An accordion starts up, followed by loud bad singing. It's too much. Her throat feels raw, her head aches.

Serge is clearing one of the work tables. "Could I... do you mind if..." she leans against the door frame, holding on to the wall to keep from falling.

At once, Serge is there at her side. "Sit," he commands. He runs down the hall to the lavatory and brings her a glass of water. "What's wrong? Are you sick?"

Marfa takes the glass with both hands and drinks. She tries to smile but only winces. She slides the kerchief off her hair, uses it to wipe her sweaty face and neck. "It's so hot. The paint fumes... I'll be all right."

As if on cue, Meti comes in dragging a huge dirty pedestal fan. "Didn't you hear me on the stairs? If the concierge hadn't helped me I'd be dead on the first landing." He glares at Marfa. "Why is she here?"

"I —"

"She —"

"Never mind. It's always one thing or another, with women. Here," he tosses her a rag from the box next to his desk. "Wipe this down. I don't want dust blowing around on the paint." He tells Serge, "I'll be at the café."

The fan starts with a reluctant whine but brings welcome relief. "Better?" Serge smiles. Marfa nods. She runs her fingers through her hair and puts her kerchief back on, tying the ends back. "You can sit until the others come back.

Or you can help me change the paper on this table," he says.

Marfa moves each person's work carefully onto their chair, along with their brushes and paints. The butcher paper, thickly crusted with multicolored drips, crackles when she and Serge start to fold it; it's too stiff to roll.

Serge brightens. "Wait. Pick up the other end. Let's put it on the floor." He brings one end over the other, drip side in, then steps on the fold to make a crease. "Again," he says. Marfa takes one corner and together they fold the piece in quarters. "Now watch this."

Serge steps onto the paper and jumps around, the dried paint snapping like firecrackers between the folds under his dancing feet. "I loved doing this when I was a kid," he tells her with mischief in his eyes. "It made Papa so angry." He steps to one side and takes her hand. "Try it."

Together they stomp and laugh until the only sound is the swish of paper against their shoes. "See?" Serge says. "Nice and flat."

He spreads fresh liner on the table. She holds the end while he cuts it to size with huge paper shears. "When did you start working?" Marfa no longer feels shy, as if their foolish escapade has made them equals.

"I hardly remember not working. Papa began painting rug canvases after he was wounded in the fighting."

"The fighting? When? Turkey was on our side, right?"

"Right. He was in the Belgian Campaign, I think. He doesn't like to talk about it, except to remind us how lucky we are the war is over." Serge sighs. "My grandparents brought him here when he was a boy. He's a Belgian citizen, but don't be fooled about his Turkish pride. That's real enough." He lifts an unfinished canvas off a chair and places it on the clean paper, centers the design easel in front of it. "He started the business at home, while the war was winding down, with a roll of canvas he found in an abandoned factory. He scrounged for whatever paint he could find, then gave the designs to my grandmother and her sister, who hooked them with wool scraps. He sold the rugs in the bazaar, or on a busy street corner."

Marfa picks up brushes and paint pots. "People bought them, during the Nazi occupation?"

"They did, or bartered for them. Nazis, too. One officer came back several times, Papa said, buying souvenirs for his wife in Düsseldorf. I don't know why I remember that. What's wrong? You look pale. Are you all right?" He cups her elbow, leads her to the nearest chair. "Maybe you should eat something."

Marfa sits down heavily at Meti's desk; her fingers tremble. She lowers her head and breathes deeply; when she looks up at him, her gaze is calm. "I'm not hungry." She pushes the dinner pail away. "When did you start painting?"

"As soon as I could hold a brush, or find paper, they tell me. Papa started me on rug canvas when I was seven. I felt important, contributing to the family income. I even liked the work, at first."

She nods. "And then?"

"Then it became too repetitive. Mechanical. I wanted freedom to make something new. To add a bee, if the spirit moved me." He grins at her. She blushes. "When the war ended, shops reopened with the help of American reconstruction money. Papa opened the studio and hired workers."

"And put you in charge of them."

"Finally, yes, last year. I had to prove I had enough authority to tell grownups what to do."

They move along the table, putting everything back in its place. Marfa takes care not to spill the paint, her hands are steady now, her movements graceful. "Your mother, did she paint too?"

"In the very beginning, at home. *Maman* didn't have much respect for peasant craft, as she called it. She stopped coming to the studio after the first month or so. They separated five, six years ago." Serge's face is impassive.

"Maybe it wasn't only about the craft," Marfa ventures, and immediately raises a hand to her mouth. "I'm sorry..."

Serge glances at her, says nothing. In the far corner, the fan rattles mightily but moves the air; the room is noticeably cooler.

"Why don't you want to go to school?" Marfa's voice is tentative, as if she needs to fill the awkward silence between them but is not sure what to say.

"I do. But not to be a lawyer or an engineer." He leans out the window. "Here they come."

"What would you study?"

"Art, of course. Literature. But Papa says I can read at home, and art school is a waste of time. He's not willing to spend money on supplies for me to ruin while I'm practicing."

"What does your mother think?"

"*Maman* would let me do anything I want, but she has no influence. And Papa is obstinate."

"I know," Marfa says, and blushes again. "I mean, I've heard how angry he gets with you."

The work stations reassembled, Marfa sits down at her

own place at the second table. She hears the workers returning, their familiar voices rising to the open windows. She lifts her canvas. The nearly finished bee is outlined in paint dots on yesterday's still-fresh butcher paper. She wants it, this fractured suggestion of an insect, more than anything she's wanted in a long time.

"Serge," she says. "Can I have this?"

"What, the canvas?"

"No. No. The paper. Just the paper."

He studies her, bemused. With a swift gesture, he picks up the shears, cuts the bee outline off the sheet, and slides a clean piece of paper under her work. They can hear the others on the stairs, their tread slow, as if reluctant to face another five hours of gentle drudgery.

Serge gives Marfa the picture. "Can I have your dinner? I don't want to go to the café."

Marfa slips the rolled-up bee picture into her bag. Just as the workers begin to file in, still talking among themselves, she lowers her voice and says, "Your name—Serge—it's not Turkish. And you call your mother *Maman* —"

"My mother is Belgian," he says, matching his tone to hers. He lifts the lid of the dinner pail and inhales. "Mmm."

Marfa picks up her brush. "My mother is dead."

7

Serge saw me shudder. I don't know what he thought, it doesn't matter. I couldn't tell if the sweat on my face was from the mid-day heat or the rising fever I tried to ignore since morning.

My mind is muddled today. Is it the fever? So many people crowding in like players on a stage, each reading from a different script.

Düsseldorf. How that word pierced through all the layers of memory and time. A wife in Düsseldorf, my Nazi said. I think he told me this before, before what came after, me at the stove cooking his breakfast, him leaning against the table admiring his polished boots. He liked to talk, even if I understood little of what he said. The necessary words—shirt, boots, kitchen, bread, potatoes, bed. Clean, hurry, come here, sleep. I knew those.

What did he say when he touched my hair, passing its curls through his fingers? Lifting it off my neck, licking the sweat there so gently I thought I would faint. Did it remind him of his wife in Düsseldorf?

We were supposed to hate them, the fascist monsters. And we did. So much senseless killing and gleeful cruelty, as if they had no mothers, no daughters or sons. Like everyone else, I had been frozen by the contempt on their faces, hot fear rippling down my back at the slightest encounter.

Why was this one different? An officer, a lieutenant, if I read the marks correctly. He must have done his duty to the Fatherland to earn those stripes. Not so young, either, the gray blending with blond, glinting in the lamplight. I could have been his teenage daughter.

He called me lovely. That I understood; he said it in my language, with loneliness in his eyes.

• • •

My mother is dead. I don't know what made me say it, as if it were recent news. My mother has been dead almost as long as I am alive; there's no particular sadness in it. You can't miss someone you never knew.

Auntie Safronia cushioned me against my father's moods. It took me years to learn why he was sharp as knives with me. I did everything wrong, some days: the way I sliced the vegetables for borsch, or folded his shirt, or milked the goat. The other times, when he simply did not see me, were worse.

That one time he hit me—for what, I don't know - Auntie Safronia said, "Never again. You hear me?"

I see the dim light in the izba, the soup kettle on the table between us, the wedge of earth-dark bread. My face stings; I couldn't see my supper through the tears. Little Auntie Safronia stood up, the better to look my seated father in the eye. "I may only be your sister, but I will drive you from this house. I will make your life a misery, if you touch this child again."

"My life? A misery? Hah." He got up and went out then, came back late. I heard him stumble against the bench and fall into bed. How old was I? Seven? I remember not daring to breathe until he started snoring. I remember everything.

When Meti raises his hand and stops short of hitting Serge, what holds him back? Is it fear of his own rage, or some long-ago promise to never hurt this child? It may be the reluctance to discipline his son in front of so many witnesses—not strangers, but people he will see day after day who will scorn him or pity his shame.

I'd like to think he's incapable of violence against Serge. His rage seems born of disappointment at his son's unwillingness to follow the path to manhood Meti has laid out for him. I want to say, open your eyes. Love the person here in front of you, not the one you imagine.

Or the one who is not, will never be there.

For all his bluster, there's something reliable about Meti. He's like a rock in the stream that stays put while the waters gather and flow. He may know nothing of tenderness, but I suspect his heart, once given, is true.

Why am I thinking this? What do I have to do with anyone's heart?

He is not wrong, not as much as Serge makes it seem. Meti has wisdom that Serge is too hasty to dismiss. Have we ever been practical when young? We reach for life's offerings like a pauper at a banquet, tempted by greed, misled by arrogance or inexperience. I know. Some of the mistakes I've made are trivial; others, the ones that haunt me, are deep and terrible.

Maybe it's the many years between our ages, but Serge is still so much a boy. A bright boy with clever ideas, a fresh way to look at the world. People want beauty, are hungry for love, he says.

And it is a new world, after the dismal years of war, the ugliness, the inhumanity and destruction. Not of buildings. There is enough stone and timber for new buildings, enough hands willing to erect them. No. That is not the tragedy. How do we recapture innocence, rebuild trust? Where do we find reason to hope the horror will never be repeated?

Serge makes me laugh like the child I never was. Stomping the paper with him was crazy and silly and wonderful. I didn't think my feet still knew how to dance, not since the last village polka back home, Petro twirling me, faster, faster, laughing, laughing. His mouth, his hands. My back against the wall of the boarded-up church, both of us knee-deep in wildflowers.

The woods were dark and wet when it came, the ground easy to dig; my hands needed no tool. It came quickly, slipped out of me with barely a twinge of pain, a little blood on the hem of my skirt. I gave it no name. It never disturbed the world with breath, content with moss and last year's pine needles for bedding, a blanket of stones.

No one knows.

I couldn't tell Auntie Safronia, and Petro was long gone. He went with the others, the red star on his cap pushed askew, rucksack on his shoulder, all of them singing like they do in war movies. As if it wasn't blood and bone for most of them at the end of that road. As if it wasn't death.

8

"She's sick again. Send her home, *Patron*, before we all die of whatever she's got." Chantal's urgent whisper carries clearly to everyone in the room.

"Who will do her work, then? You?" Meti is impassive. "Bad enough we lost Elise last week."

"Elise will be back once the baby is born, and she took work to do at home."

"I don't know how you talked me into that. She probably has the whole family at it, dabbing away like it's some kind of game. God only knows how that will turn out." He speaks in a normal voice, loud, not caring who hears.

"Well, I can't afford to lose my pay. I have no children, but most everyone here does." She flicks a hand in Marfa's direction. "We don't need to bring her sickness to our families. Send her home."

Marfa shrinks in her seat. She has moved to the table at the end, with Elise's empty place between her and one of the middle-aged women. She tries to stifle a cough and fails. She runs from the studio, hands tented over her mouth, her nose.

"We're all in this room all day. We use the same lavatory. At least open a window to clear the air." Chantal is almost shouting now.

Meti looks tired. "It's January," he says. "I'm not paying to heat the street."

"Well, then —" She stands up, feet apart, hands on hips.

"Enough, Chantal. Don't bring your bazaar manners in here. Get back to work."

In the hallway, Marfa waits until her coughing subsides. The lavatory water pitcher is an old, ornate piece painted with cherubs and faded pink roses, enamel chipped around the upper edge. It makes her think of a Victorian birthday card. She tips water into the basin, just enough to submerge her hands and splash her face. In the dingy mirror, its pocked surface etched with spidery cracks, her cheeks look flushed with fever, her eyes huge, dull. In the unheated room, the water feels icy on her hot skin. She shivers with her whole body.

She drinks from her cupped hand, wipes the sleeve of her dress over her face. If she stays away more than five minutes, she knows Meti will reduce her pay. "Please, not this week," she says. "Not this week."

The atmosphere in the studio is charged with tension. Meti glances at the clock on his desk when Marfa returns to work, but says nothing. Serge comes in trailing cold air; there's snow in his hair and on the shoulders of his coat. "What happened? Did somebody die?" He looks around the room. Everyone is silent, intent on their work. Meti looks to be deep in thought. The radio crackles with static, the fire in the iron stove hisses and pops.

"Not yet," Chantal says. Marfa pulls at the sleeves of her sweater, tugging the cuffs down over her hands, leaving only her fingers exposed.

"Why is it so cold in here? We can't be out of coal, I just brought some on Monday." Serge tosses a scoopful of fuel into the stove and clangs the door shut. "No wonder people are getting sick."

Marfa's chest heaves with fresh spasms of bronchial coughing. She struggles to catch her breath, but doesn't dare leave her seat again. "Go home, Marfa," Serge says. "Go home and go to bed." Meti starts to protest, then seems to change his mind. Marfa shakes her head and keeps painting with slow careful movements. She hopes no one notices the trembling of her brush.

"It's Thursday. I'll pay you for the rest of the day," Serge puts a hand on the back of her chair. "Go home."

Meti looks up. "Not with my money."

"No, Papa. With mine."

"Yours? Since when do you have money to throw around?"

"You pay me little enough, that's true. But I have money. I sold a poem."

"Really? And now you're so rich you can pass out favors to the less fortunate. Big man, you are. Poet." Meti spits out the word. "Maybe we should clear all this out and write poetry instead."

"Not rich. But I can do this, today." Serge keeps his tone even, refusing to take the bait. "Marfa's a good worker."

"They're all good workers!" Meti flings an arm out wide. "Why don't you sell another poem and pay them all?"

"Because she's the one who's sick," Serge says quietly. "And she'll have three days to recover by Monday."

"Good idea, Serge," Chantal cuts in. "The sooner she leaves, the better for the rest of us."

Marfa covers her paints and cleans her brush. She gathers up her things and puts on her coat, trying to make as little disturbance as possible. When Serge holds out the money for the week, she takes it. It's hard to tell if her face is red from fever or embarrassment.

One of the women who wears the Muslim scarf takes a small jar from her bag and tucks it into Marfa's coat pocket. "You cough all week. This is honey, from my sister in Holland. Good for cough."

"Oh," Marfa says. "That is so kind, Sofia. I never thought... you... we don't talk... I..." She walks quickly from the room and down the stairs into the street, hooding her winter scarf over her head against the thickly falling snow.

9

Marfa's shoes are soaked before she reaches the corner. The Place du Jeu de Balle is deserted, its grimy cobblestones concealed under a sheet of fresh snow. A trail of footprints stitches its way from one of the houses to the door of the church. The mid-afternoon light is dim as twilight. She cuts diagonally through the square, heading for the streetcar stop on the boulevard.

The wind hits her as soon as she enters the wide avenue. It bites at her face and tears at her coat, flings bucketfuls of snow in all directions. The dormant fountain in the center of the thoroughfare is encased in ice; long fat icicles snap and crash from the statuary into the empty basin below. It is beautiful, but no one notices. People make their way, hunched into their overcoats, hand on hat, eager for the shelter of home.

Marfa has lived in the city long enough to know the easterly North Sea wind is less strong closer to the buildings, but the drifts are deeper there and walking is more difficult. She stumbles along the middle of the sidewalk, clutches her coat tighter, pulls the end of her scarf over most of her face against the needles of shooting snow.

She's hardly aware of her fever, of the blood throbbing in her ears, the tightness in her chest. When she raises a bare hand to wipe away the snow plastered to her eyelashes, she sees the streetcar, still half a long block away, disappear into the storm. She cries out. No one hears her. A fist of wind howls with maniacal laughter, catches her in the back and slams her to the ground.

She can't breathe or move. After a moment - or an hour - strong hands take her under the elbows and pull her up, brushing the snow off her back, her head. She gasps for air and lets out a sob, raises her eyes through frozen tears. "M... M... Meti," she stammers.

"Foolish woman," he shouts to be heard over the storm. "You keep close to the buildings when it's windy. Everybody knows that."

"I... I..." Marfa tries to respond through clattering teeth. Her body shakes uncontrollably.

Meti guides her toward the wall of a department store. She bends her head and stands swaying, one hand pressed to the wall. "Come," he says. He leads her down a side street toward the lighted, steamed up windows of a small café.

The man behind the counter, in shirtsleeves and an embroidered woolen vest, says, "Hello, Mehmet. How long since we've seen snow like this? They're saying —"

"Bring a pot of tea, and a pack of Murads, Selim," Meti interrupts, returning the greeting with a nod. "And soup," he adds, "for her. Take off your coat," he tells Marfa. "You'll warm up faster."

Marfa is still shaking, the buttons on her coat will not yield to her wet cold fingers. She drops her arms and wails.

"Arggh," Meti growls. He unbuttons the coat and drapes it over a chair near the iron stove. "What kind of coat is this for winter? It's wet through." He taps the pack of cigarettes against the table, takes one out and lights it. Inhales. "You people. It's a wonder you're still alive."

36

The tea smells faintly of oranges; it is hot and strong and sweet. The first sip scorches Marfa's throat and tongue. She wraps her hands over the tiny cup, and lets the heat warm her fingers, feeling the tremors subside. Meti greets the other customers by name. They are all men, Marfa notices; they all smoke. Some read newspapers. One pair face each other over a chess game. The radio plays a melancholy Turkish tune, flutes and a stringed instrument that reminds her of a balalaika. She feels out of place, but grateful to be indoors.

"Thank you, *Patron*," she says. "But why..."

He shrugs. "I needed cigarettes."

The shirt-sleeved man brings a plate of soup, thick with barley and vegetables around a gristly lamb shank. Marfa eats, slowly at first, then with gusto, cleaning the meat off the bone, leaving it bare in the empty plate. "That was good. Thank you."

"Stop thanking me. I know what you eat. Potatoes and stale bread. Kasha. Who can live on that?"

Marfa doesn't answer. She reaches to touch the scarf draped over her coat on the chair. It's steaming a little, the ends dripping onto the floor. "It's still damp," she says.

"You're not going out there in those wet clothes," Meti decrees.

She's not about to argue. The hot food and warm air have loosened the congestion in her head, making her nose run, aggravating her cough. She rummages in her satchel for a handkerchief and finds none. "Here," Meti pulls his out of his pocket. "How did you ever survive the war? You're hopeless."

Marfa blows her nose. "Without handkerchiefs."

Meti orders another pot of tea. "Who made that scarf? You?"

"No. I don't know how. My aunt made it for me just before... before I left home." She feels the fever returning. Her head aches. She's suddenly sleepy.

"Home. Ukraine?"

"Yes. A little village near the Romanian border."

And then she's talking, talking like never before; she doesn't know why. About Auntie Safronia sitting in her old wooden chair in the warm corner near the stove, under the tarnished *ikona* of Saint Nicholas, making the scarf out of whatever was left in her yarn basket. See? Red and yellow and blue.

"She liked to hum, old hymns, I think. She had me baptized after my mother died. I don't know anything about that, about the old religion. I never saw the inside of a church or met a priest until Germany. Regensburg. Until my friend Galina and her mother took me along and asked me to hold baby Katyusha, be her godmother."

"I remember them," Meti says. "A beautiful girl, Galina. Beautiful hair."

"Yes." Marfa tries to smooth her own disheveled curls. "The service was lovely, but odd. I didn't know the prayers, had to repeat the words slowly, like a schoolgirl. Strange words in a dense language I didn't know, like Russian and Ukrainian mixed together, sounding like ancient poetry. Auntie Safronia tried to teach me some prayers when I was small, but I was too impatient and not interested in learning about the old ways."

"Wasn't that dangerous, if people got caught?"

Marfa nods. "The Soviet way was the new religion.

People had been sent away for no reason. And you know how unpredictable children are when it comes to keeping secrets. The less they know, the better." She feels dizzy, her mind swirling with memories, impressions magnified by the fire in her brain.

She can't stop talking. She tells Meti about the funeral for one of the old men in the village. How the horses had all been taken by the collective, or eaten by the starving people, in the hungry years. About the women in black dresses and colorful kerchiefs walking behind the donkey wagon, chanting in thin sad voices. "I thought they looked like crows out of a fairy tale, crows with flowers on their heads." She smiles. Meti smiles back.

She tells him how some of the women faltered over the words of the burial service, but Auntie Safronia and the grandmothers sounded confident. How one even kept time, her calloused hand marking the beat while the others followed.

"Weren't they afraid—having the funeral, singing hymns outdoors?"

"Of course they were afraid. But they were wartime women. They may have seemed timid, but they found ways to get what they needed. They needed to do this." Marfa sips her tepid tea, its sweetness soothing her inflamed throat.

"I never thought much about what the war was like for women," Meti admits. "Or about what it was like at home, while we were busy fighting. To keep them safe, I thought." He rubs a hand over his face, shakes another cigarette out of the pack.

"This is before the war you knew," she answers. "Some of those women lived through the Great War and the

Revolution, and then civil war and famine. And then the Nazi occupation. When were they ever safe? Never."

They sit silent a while, listening to the muted click of chess pieces on the board, the rustling of newspapers. On the radio, a woman's nasal voice sings a repetitive refrain. Marfa lays her head down on her arms, closes her eyes. After a few minutes, Meti gets up and goes to the window. "The snow has stopped," the shirt-sleeved man says. "But not the wind."

10

Funny that he asked about the scarf.

There's Auntie Safronia trying to teach me crochet, but I can't sit still long enough to make my fingers do the stitches. She is impatient. How will you live, if you don't know how to do anything? Me all sass and ten-year-old bravado: I know how to cook! And didn't I? Not just porridge and potatoes.

Precious times, those evenings, her hook moving through the yarn as if with its own purpose, me with a schoolbook or some mending. I knew how to do that.

The Germans take the young ones first. Auntie says, I'm not sixteen, like you. They need workers, not weak old women. She squeezes my hand, blesses me. No time for crying. No time for fear.

I climb in the truck with the other girls. A soldier tosses a flaming torch onto our little house, then jumps into the back of the truck. The grim smile he gives me when I catch his eye stays with me in my nightmares.

Auntie Safronia stands in the road, arms at her sides, the sod on the roof smolders behind her. She looks shrunken, lost. Alone like me in a hostile world. My heart aches.

All I have left is this moth-eaten scarf. I don't know how to pray.

It was like the river, that wind, pulling, shoving. Merciless, mocking. The river that took what it wanted.

Tolik. My own.

Meti walked me all the way home. The streetcar never came. He held my arm at the icy patches. Thank you, I said at the door. He watched me start up the stairs. How far? His voice boomed through the empty hall. Four flights, I said. Attic. And sat down on the third step, my head spinning.

11

"No men in the room." The landlady steps out on the landing, blocking the way upstairs. "I told you that the first day."

"Step aside, woman," Meti says. "Can't you see she's sick?"

"And I suppose you're the doctor." She turns to shake a finger in Marfa's face. "If he's not out of here in five minutes, you're on the street, *chérie*, where you belong. And don't think I've forgotten about the rent. Tomorrow's Friday." She looks like a puppet show character in a house dress and worn-out slippers. Only the rolling pin is missing. Marfa starts to laugh but ends up coughing instead, holding on to the rail with both hands.

"Come on." Meti slips a hand under Marfa's arm and starts up the stairs. "Come on." He brushes past the woman on the landing. "Bring her tea and bread in the morning," he says, and adds, "I'll pay," when she starts to open her mouth.

The last flight of stairs, to the fourth floor, is too narrow for two people. "I can do it now," Marfa says. "You go. You've done so much already. Here, give her this." She counts some money out of her change purse. "For the rent, so she'll give me a few days' peace."

Meti waits to leave until she's reached the door of her room. "Go to bed and stay there."

The next three days pass in a haze of fitful sleep and long hours of debilitating wakefulness. Someone has moved her table closer to the bed. From time to time, a cup of tea and wedge of brown bread appear; once, a hardboiled egg, which she cannot force down her constricted throat. Marfa guesses it's the landlady, who else? But why is she suddenly kind? Meti, of course, with his fierce demeanor. No doubt the persuasion of his money had more than a little to do with the woman's new-found solicitude.

Marfa stumbles down to the third-floor lavatory. She can smell the sickness on her skin; her hair hangs in greasy locks around her face. *I look like death.* She starts to wash with a damp towel, but gives up, exhausted, after wiping her face and neck. Back in her room, she adds a few lumps of coal to the fire in the stove.

She is just crawling into bed when the landlady's twelve-year-old daughter comes in with a fresh cup of tea. "*Maman* says you should go to the clinic, to get medicine. It's free, for poor people."

"I know," Marfa croaks in a strained whisper. She doesn't say that by the time she gets the strength to get to the clinic, she will no longer need the medicine. "How is it outside? More snow?"

The child replaces the empty cup with the hot one. "No more snow. Too bad, I liked it! The wind has died down, but it's very cold." She puts a vial of pills and a glass of water next to the tea. "A man came and brought you these. Aspirin for the grippe and the fever, he said."

"An older man, with a dark mustache?"

"No, a young one. Nice looking." She giggles and backs out of the room, closing the door behind her.

Serge. She shakes two pills out of the vial, gets them down. Sleeps.

Monday morning dawns with intermittent sun between shifting clouds. Far below her window she hears the vendors from outside the city push their farm carts through the street, calling out their wares. Cabbages. Potatoes. Turnips. Walnuts. Anything else that keeps in their root cellars until the new harvest. It's a timeless singsong that hovers at the back of sleep: the voices rise and fall in an echo that lingers long after they have passed by. Marfa looks out to see women come out of their houses, a basket in one hand and change purse in the other, coats thrown hastily over their nightgowns. Some have bandanas around their heads, concealing curling papers. The new week has begun.

She drinks off yesterday's cold tea and gets dressed. It's an effort, but she must go. No work, no pay, no food. No room, either, if she gets behind on the rent.

Out on the street, the cold slices through her coat and sweater in minutes. What sun there is looks pale and gives no warmth. The cough returns, along with the fever, the ache in her arms and legs. After a few meters, she retraces her steps. Under the blanket with her clothes on she pulls the sweater tight around her neck until the shivering stops. For the first time since her illness began, she thinks she might die.

Time passes. Is it Tuesday? Marfa's head is heavy on the pillow, her mind full of restless dreams. Multicolored dots on brown butcher paper dance behind her eyes. It's hot, the fan is blowing grotesque oversized insects around the room. No, it's cold, the stove glows red, something boils furiously in a coal bucket. Hammering. Chantal is pounding nails into the table, singing along with the radio. Everyone keeps painting, heads down, their brushes gone wild, each canvas covered with random smears.

It's not hammering. It's footsteps on the stairs. A knock. The door opens. "Meti," she says, barely awake. "It's you."

"Keep that door open," the landlady calls from below. "I've got my eye on you."

"*Oui, Madame.*" Meti shakes his head and laughs. "Some imagination. You look better. Dreadful, but better." He sets the bag he's carrying down on the table. "I was going to send one of the women, but they're all afraid of getting sick. And Serge has a bit of a cough himself."

"And you? You're not afraid to get sick?"

"Me? I'm a tough old bull. Nothing sticks to me."

He starts removing jars and parcels, holds each one up and names it before putting it down. "Moroccan flatbread from the men. They make it themselves, you know." Wild strawberry jam. A tin of potted meat. A small loaf of honey bread encrusted with sugar crystals, a smiling boy and girl on the cellophane wrapper. Powdered milk. A piece of real butter wrapped in waxy white paper. "Everyone put something in," he says, sitting down in the only chair.

Meti picks up a white box printed with an exuberant crowing rooster. "Corn flakes, from America. I don't know how they eat this stuff, it tastes like cardboard. Maybe that's why they send it here, because they think we're so hungry we'll eat anything."

"We should be grateful for the American relief. I mean, we were that hungry, weren't we?"

"After they bombed our cities. Yes, I know. To stop the Germans and win the war." Meti looks at her over his glasses. "It wasn't pure altruism, that relief. It was a message to the Bolsheviks, who understand how to control people through food supply."

"I know."

"But you're right. It was a generous impulse from a country whose farms and factories were unscarred by bombing. Those people know nothing of the terror of war. We should be grateful, as you say." He reaches into the bag again. A knitted hat. A book of poems by Verlaine. "From Serge. Now that's useful."

Marfa smiles. She sits up, her eyes wide at the bounty before her. "I can't believe... everyone... Chantal... they never even talk to me."

"And you? Do you talk to them? You sit like a mouse in your corner, saying nothing."

"What should I say?" Marfa looks genuinely baffled.

"You can keep your secrets, whatever they are. Say a word about the weather, the song on the radio, anything. Speak up. We're just people, Marfa. Even Chantal — she's mostly bluster anyway. She shelters stray animals, cats and dogs, and gives them away. Did you know that? No, how could you."

"I—"

"Never mind. I didn't come here to lecture you. Here, eat my veal stew, it's still warm." He puts a dinner pail in her hands, gives her a fork. While she eats, Meti refills her coal bucket from a paper sack he had left at the door.

Marfa tears off a piece of flatbread to wipe up the last of the sauce. "You cook?" Her voice is feeble, tremulous. It's as if she doesn't know how to respond to all the unexpected attention.

"Better than my wife ever did."

When he turns to go, his glance catches the stippled bee

design tacked to the wall between a calendar from a commercial bakery and a picture of roadside wildflowers torn from a magazine. "Huh," he grunts.

Marfa is looking out the window. "Clouds," she says. "Maybe more snow, or rain." She looks at him for a long silent moment. "Please thank everyone for me. I'll come back ..." she coughs, hard. "... maybe tomorrow."

"Come back next week. Oh, I almost forgot this." He takes some money out of his pocket. "Everyone put something in. I can't pay you for not working, but this should cover your room. Should I give it to the witch downstairs?" He grins. "No, that could be trouble for you. Better do it yourself."

Marfa hesitates, then says in a rush, as if afraid she'll lose her courage, "Why are you doing this, *Patron*, for me? The city is full of women who need work. Why, Meti?" She is looking at him, her eyes momentarily unclouded by fever. "No one collected anything for Elise and her baby. Not that I know."

"The women will do something after it's born. And she has family, a husband," he mumbles, avoiding her direct gaze.

"How did you know I didn't? I never said..."

"You didn't have to," he shrugs.

And then he's gone.

12

I'm glad Serge didn't come up with the aspirin. To see me like this—it's unthinkable.

Am I vain?

The German never saw me in the morning, each of us in our own beds while the night was still dark and the moon high in the sky. Me combed and dressed, his breakfast ready and the washing or ironing started by the time he rose.

He had soft hands, the German. Gentle lips. He never scolded me; I gave him no reason. Still, he could have.

You're a good girl, he said, but I can't take you with me. I have a wife in Düsseldorf. Two boys. The war is over, I must go.

Not soon enough—the British came and took him away. You're fine, they told me, it's over. Go to the DP camp.

But it had only begun, the trouble.

We women tend to look for men like our fathers to love. I read it in a French magazine. Elle, I think it was. My father, whose only words for me were harsh ones, who would have beaten me if he hadn't been afraid of his sister. If he hadn't disappeared for good before I turned twelve. The thought of loving a man like that makes me shudder, and also laugh.

Agh, what do I know? Auntie Safronia said once, at harvest time, watching him walk away to the fields, his shoulders hunched, head down: He loved your mother. Couldn't get enough of her.

Who knows what breaks a man.

What kind of man would Petro have become? Is it hard labor and hard drinking that kill the joy men are born with? Oh. The sweet pressure of his thighs stayed with me night and day, long after he was gone.

Were you afraid, Petro, in the fighting? Or were you too full of life? You who are forever young, eternally beautiful. Did you remember me?

The idleness of lying in bed all these days, looking at the ceiling or out the window at the silent sky, fills my head with too many pointless questions.

So many ghosts.

It must be the fever.

13

"You have family? Children?" Sofia moves her work aside, spreads a kitchen towel on the table before opening her dinner pail. It's too cold to go outside.

Marfa doesn't answer right away. She's still not used to talking to the other workers, in spite of the noticeable thaw in the room. Since her illness, everyone nods and some even smile at her, and for this she is grateful. But there isn't much conversation, and that is a relief, in its own way. In the years since the war's end, people don't ask about each other's experiences. What is there to say? We suffered. It was horrific. It's in the past.

What does she have to talk about? Nothing has happened in her life since Galina and Filip, her only friends, left for America. Her days are dreary, each one like the last, each one a tedious exercise in survival. Nothing to look forward to in another day as empty as this one.

But Sofia has warm eyes and looks interested.

"Family." Marfa keeps her voice low, reluctant to broadcast her answer. "No. That is, I don't think so."

Sofia inclines her head to one side, waiting. Marfa wonders what life is like for Muslim women, whether they speak openly at home. She sees them on the streetcar or at the open-air market, often in twos and threes, surrounded by children, talking only among themselves. The direct question takes her by surprise; she's not sure how much of a reply is expected.

"My mother died when I was born," she offers. She balances her dinner on her lap, eats carefully, not too fast.

"That is sad, not to know your mother."

"My aunt raised me. My father's sister." Marfa looks up. "Maybe she's still alive."

They eat in silence. "Stalin is dead, but getting a letter from the west might put her in danger," she adds after a while. "If she ever received it."

The studio fills with mingled food aromas and the ping and scrape of cutlery on metal dishes. Sofia looks sympathetic. She takes an apple from her pocket, offers Marfa half. The men in cloth caps have finished their meal and gone out for their daily walk. Serge sits at the desk, sketching. When Meti steps out, Chantal turns up the radio.

"And your father?" Chantal asks, casual. She takes a cigarette from the pack on Meti's desk.

Marfa is startled by the question—whether by its intimate boldness or by its coming from Chantal, it's hard to say. "He... he left to work on the hydro-electric dam, on the Dnieper river, when the collective failed. I was twelve." She gathers up her dinner things. "Many men went. He never came back."

"Not many do," Chantal muses. She opens the window a crack and blows a stream of smoke outside. The room is suddenly noisy with talk and, at one table, laughter.

"What a hen house," Meti says from the doorway. He sounds gruff but not angry. The men in cloth caps come in behind him and go right to work. The younger one startles Marfa with a friendly passing glance. The women pick up their brushes. Meti waves at the radio. "Turn that down,

Chantal. Break's over."

It takes Marfa another few days to approach Sofia. It's still winter, but the air is balmy; some of the women walk to the flea market, coats open to the breeze. "Sofia, the honey you gave me, it was so good." She blushes. "I should have thanked you before."

"My sister has bees, and many flowers, in Holland. Also herbs: lavender, rosemary, mint." The older woman smiles and adjusts her scarf. "Maybe that's why I like your bee picture."

"Oh," Marfa laughs. "I was afraid Meti would throw me out, right then. I don't know why he didn't." She pauses. Her fingers brush the corner of the other woman's scarf. "The head covering you wear—what do you call it, in your language?"

"It is called hijab." After a moment, Sofia says, "Meti is a good man. He tries to hide it with his scolding and shouting, but we all know. When my Rahima was sick, he paid to send her to a seaside camp for a month. Imagine."

They stroll among the vendors, talking, looking at other people's cast-offs, neither of them tempted to buy. Sofia tells Marfa that Muslim law or custom requires women to wear the scarf—hijab—outdoors or in mixed gatherings.

"Who makes the law?"

"Men do," she said. "Men make the law, but women bear the thread of life. Women make the home."

"In my village, the women wore scarves or kerchiefs all day, sunrise to bedtime," Marfa says. "In the fields, everyone's head was covered, children, too; men and boys wore caps to shield them from the sun. No law about that, just necessity. My auntie said in the old times, women had to cover their heads in church, while men stood bareheaded in a separate section. She said the sight of a woman's hair distracts men from their prayers."

Sofia nods.

Who is the weaker then? Who needs protecting? Marfa wonders.

Something on the ground, next to a pile of children's clothes, partly concealed by a scattering of tattered magazines, catches Marfa's eye. It's a phonograph record, Red Army Choir, traditional Russian songs. She picks it up, turns it over and over in her hands. The men on the jacket stand shoulder to shoulder, row after row in pressed dress uniform, caps just so. They look healthy, radiant. Marfa scans the list of selections.

"What is that? Is it good?" Sofia glances sideways at the record.

Marfa puts it back on the ground. "Oh. Nothing. Just some songs."

They walk a few steps behind the others back to the studio. "How many children, Sofia?" Marfa is looking down as if mesmerized by the motion of their feet. Out of the corner of her eye, she sees her companion raise her hand, fingers splayed.

"Five. All girls."

"Five! How can you work?" The words are out before Marfa can hold them back.

"They are not so small. The older ones watch the young ones. And you?"

Marfa pulls her coat closed though the sun is still warm. She wraps her arms around herself and whispers, "No. No children."

Sofia touches Marfa on the arm. "My name is Safya; only the Belgians cannot remember."

The rest of the day goes fast. The sunlight has lifted everyone's spirits; it seems to have energized the very brushes, made the paint flow on canvas almost of its own volition. By evening, the street is chilly. The workers leave, each with a separate destination, returning to obligations, families.

Marfa is not eager to see her solitary room, with its dark corners and narrow bed. She takes her time, stops to admire a tray of pastries in the bakery window, buys a hard baguette for tomorrow's breakfast. She's almost reached the flea market square when she hears footsteps behind her, hurrying. Her name.

She turns. "Serge. What—"

"Here, this is for you." He's panting a little, his face shiny with sweat. "I saw you looking at it. I thought you'd like to have it."

He holds out the phonograph record of the Red Army Choir. Marfa is momentarily speechless. "I... I don't... I can't..." She recovers, takes in his open expression, his obvious desire to please. "Thank you, Serge."

14

These men, Meti, Serge, they puzzle me. Is it just solicitude, is that possible? I don't know if such a thing exists between men and women, or if everyone feels the tension that drqws us together while getting in the way of real understanding.

What does Chantal know about the ones who don't return?

Everything has a price. At the flea market, no one gives things away, no matter how shabby they are.

What am I worth? What do they see when they look at me?

All the songs on the record are familiar ones: Katyusha, Dark Eyes, Kalinka, The Cliff, Roads. The men, singing. That afternoon concert in the park. Germany, after the war. Was it Schwarzenberg? The glorious sound they made shook the leaves on the trees. So many of us, thousands, standing listening, letting the voices take us home.

Did singing save them? Or did they also serve, leaving an arm, two fingers, a booted foot, a wounded spirit on the battlefield. The sacrifice, the waste.

We sang these old songs. The funny ones and the sad ones, and the ones about love. And aren't they all about love, isn't everything, really, about love?

When I hold the record up to the lamp, I can see the scratch. If I had a phonograph, the voices would catch; interrupted or silenced, they would trip over each other, fade away. In my head they sing perfectly, in virile harmony, forever. It's better that way.

Sofia—Safya—asked me about children. And there he was in my arms, my mother's old shawl wrapped around his little body, his head hot against my chest. Tolik. Quiet. Trusting. I should have been more afraid of the wind and the night and the water.

I should have died.

Five, she said. A good mother. She would never lose one, no matter what.

15

Marfa cannot at first remember what brought her to Meti's apartment this May night.

Ah, yes. The papers. The ones that have lain in disarray on Meti's desk for weeks. Day after day, he either ignores them, spreading the newspaper on top, heedless of the ashes his perpetually lit cigarette scatters on the growing mound. Or he pushes the papers around, first one way then another, pretending to sort them. He sighs and walks away to stare out the window, with barely a word to anyone. The workers respond to the tension by working on the canvas in front of them with renewed concentration.

Serge has been out since early that morning. He'd seemed preoccupied when he collected the finished pieces and slipped them into his portfolio. They heard him clatter down the stairs as if eager to leave the studio behind. "You know he signed up for an art class, at the Lysée," Chantal whispers without looking up from her work.

Marfa cleans the scarlet paint from her brush and switches to Prussian blue. She nods. Everyone knows except Meti.

Serge returns well after midday.

"Well?" Meti eyes the portfolio. It looks to be as full as when he left.

Serge shakes his head. "Not much. But I heard the department store is adding a needlework section. We should go talk to them."

"You go. That's your job. I have to deal with all this." He passes a hand through his hair and waves at the mess on his desk. "Maybe we should slow down a little," he says, dropping his voice but still speaking loud enough for everyone to hear. "But all these people... they need the work."

"You know best, Papa."

"No. I thought so, but no, I don't know best anymore."

"We could open a booth on the Grand' Place near the cloth vendors, on Saturdays." Serge sounds tentative.

"And undercut the shops we've been selling to for five, six years? That's stupid, Serge." He stirs the bills and invoices, gathers them into an untidy pile. "Bring me these tonight, at home, after you close. I'm going to the café."

After Meti leaves, Serge walks around, looking over the workers' shoulders, exchanging a word here and there. It isn't supervision; everyone knows what to do. When he gets to Marfa, she says softly, "How was your class?"

"Excellent." He leans in with a smile equal parts embarrassment and delight. "I guess everyone knows."

Marfa puts a finger to her lips. "Not everyone."

For the rest of the day, Serge sits at the desk, engrossed in writing and sketching. He doesn't see the note that passes from hand to hand; he doesn't see each person read it and add their name. When he looks up, the paper disappears into Chantal's pocket.

It's an hour before closing when the boy bursts into the room, red-faced and breathless. "Serge, you must come. There's been an accident. Your mother —"

"What? Where? Is she all right?"

"No, she's hurt. You must come now."

pot.

He stares at the papers on the edge of the table. Sighs. "I don't know how this will end. The paint supplier is threatening court—and after only three months! I can't pull money out of the air, but without paint..." He scratches his head, picks up the top invoice, puts it down again.

Marfa dries her hands on a linen towel. "Listen, *Patron*. Don't tell Chantal I told you this. We all agreed to work an hour or two less every day until things get better. That way no one needs to be dismissed and the work can continue at a slower pace." She wipes the stove, puts the plates and forks away. "She'll tell you tomorrow. We all signed."

"Are you crazy? You think I don't know how you all struggle? Especially you women. What woman would work if she didn't have to?"

Marfa's face flushes red. "What would you have us do, sit and play solitaire all day? I come from a farm village. Everyone works one way or another until they die."

"I know, I know. Don't get upset. My family were city folk, three generations of poor people trying to scrape out a living, believing things would soon change. And they did, but not for us."

Marfa stirs honey into her tea, floats a thin round of lemon on top. "When was this, your family leaving Turkey?"

"1912. I was eight."

They sip their tea, dipping windmill-shaped almond cookies into their cups.

"More?"

"No." She smiles. "Thank you for dinner. It was delicious." She takes a deep breath. "Please think about what I told you. If you close the studio, we're all in trouble, all of us out of work at once, and you'll still have these bills to pay."

Meti doesn't reply. He gets up to put the tea things in the sink. Marfa is aware of him standing behind her chair. She feels unsettled by his closeness, but also strangely calm. He sets his hands on the back of the chair, says her name.

She looks up. He touches her shoulder; the pressure is light but firm, sending warmth from his hand deep into her body. She shudders, unable to move. His kiss is brief but insistent.

"No. Meti, no." She stares at her hands clasped in her lap. "I have to go now."

"It's late," he says. "I'll walk you to the streetcar."

"No need, I can manage. Good night."

Marfa walks as if drunk, her head swims. Confusion edged with panic, and something else, buried but not forgotten, is urgently awake. She's gone around the square twice before she finds the street again. When she knocks, Meti lets her in.

16

He is gentle and also strong. I like the hardness, the bones beneath the skin, his chest against me, shoulder blades under my hands. The legs supple, muscular.

I didn't know I missed the touching. Wanted the kiss. But oh, yes, I did.

Why did you come back? His hands in my hair. Nice hands, a little rough, the fingers long and shapely. I answered, later.

You gave me money, I said.

When you were sick? That was from—

So you said, but I know it was from you, and maybe Serge. No one in that room has money to give away.

He wasn't pleased, his mouth a straight line, neither denying nor affirming my guess. It doesn't matter, I said. I needed it. Maybe I should be proud, proud and poorer than I am now. But I'm not. I never have been. I do what I'm told, take what I'm given. Like that first day.

The first day? Heavens, woman, that was pocket change. You looked like you hadn't eaten in a week.

Not my pocket. And maybe I hadn't. But there had to be a price. Nothing—

He sat up, put his feet on the floor, his back to me. Rigid with anger. Is that what you think? That I... I bought you with a few coins? That I've waited for the chance to claim my right, like some kind of slave master, some feudal lord of the manor?

I wanted to stroke his back, relieve the tension. Those

smooth shoulders, and the dense hair running down to his buttocks along the backbone, glinting with gray in the light from the other room. I didn't dare.

Tears slipped down my temples into the pillow. I couldn't stop them. After a while he half-turned to me. I'm a man, he said. I like women. I liked you from the first day. The way you held yourself, asked for the job. I don't know what you've been through, but it hasn't been easy, and you're still standing. Your eyes, they see everything, give nothing away. There's a mystery about you, an untold story. And yes, a pull, an animal attraction, too.

He lit a cigarette, lay down. Many quiet minutes, side by side without touching. My tears dried. I even dozed a little.

That officer, the one you worked for. Did you think I was like him? No, don't tell me anything. I'm not a sensitive man. I'm cut from rough timber, unpolished. But I'm no Nazi. How could you even think .... He stubbed his cigarette into the ashtray and looked at me. How could you? The anger was gone.

You're wrong, I said. You are a sensitive man.

The next kiss was better, deeper.

17

"How is your mother?" Marfa uncovers her paint pots, stirs the green with the tip of her brush. "Was she badly hurt?"

Serge seems surprised by the question. "No, nothing serious."

"Someone said it was a delivery wagon that hit her," Chantal says. "Is that true?"

"No. How do these rumors start?" Serge snaps. "It was a taxi, and it barely touched her. She fell down, though, and bruised her knees, her arm." He holds up his elbow to demonstrate. "At the clinic, they treated her with mercurochrome and sent her home." He shook his head. "*Maman* gets a little—"

"Hysterical," Meti put in. "Mercurochrome. She could have done that at home. Now she's walking around like a child who fell off a bicycle, showing off her red-tinted scratches like battle scars." He waves a dismissive hand. "You should have known better than to go running, playing into her drama." He glances at Marta and looks away. She bends to her work, her cheeks rosy.

Serge makes for the door. "She's my mother. It could have been fatal, or at least serious."

"Where are you going? It's too early for deliveries."

"To the café."

"You don't like the café."

"Not yours. The French one."

• • •

A week passes. Meti sits slumped in his chair, the workers' proposal in his hand. "All right," he says. "I accept your offer. But only one hour each, in the evening, until things get better." He gestures at the window. "We can all enjoy a little more of this fine weather."

It's payday. The workers file past the desk to receive their envelopes. He thanks each one, addressing them in a low voice, asking about their families. Marfa is last in line. "Look," he says. "I ran out of small bills." He sends Serge to the newsstand for change.

They wait. Since that night, they have barely spoken to one another. Marfa knows, feels, when he's looking at her, but avoids his gaze. She can't imagine what she might say, can't help wondering about the women in the room. Has he... have they... Chantal...? Is there something everyone knows, like Serge's secret art class, but no one talks about? Is she the last of many, or the only one to succumb?

"Can you come by tonight? Will you?" Meti looks her full in the face.

They hear the street door open, Serge's steps on the stairs. Marfa nods.

"In about an hour," Meti says.

They all leave together. Meti locks up, pockets the key.

"Good night." He walks briskly away.

"Aren't you going home? It's the other direction," Serge calls after him.

"Halal butcher shop." Meti throws the words over his shoulder. "I may be a bad Muslim, but I like good meat."

Serge is about to go his own way when Marfa says, suddenly reckless, "Where is the French café? Is it far?"

Serge blinks, smiles. "It's the other side of the square, near the boulevard. I can show you."

18

What did I expect? When he let me in, the first time, did I think I'd find the same disorder as his perpetually messy desk? Dirty dishes, unmade bed, clothes strewn about—that would not have surprised me.

Instead, some reading material on a chair, two shirts to be laundered. Floor swept, window washed; no dust or cobwebs anywhere. I notice these things, don't I. Cleaning up after others has been the constant in my journey.

The kitchen calendar—a Venetian gondolier against the backdrop of an ornate cathedral looks whimsical and exotic on the bare walls. Nothing else, no pictures or photographs or mementos in the room; only the essentials for a quiet life.

Bedroom, in the morning: a folded towel on the dresser, a soap dish, a few toiletries. A comb. A small square mirror hung from a nail. In the far corner, a leather suitcase on top of a narrow wardrobe. A low bookcase within arm's reach of the bed. The Turkish rug on the wall next to the bookcase harmonizes with the wool blanket colors—the same reds, browns, dark green. No flowers here, no fanciful insects or birds. An existence without complications, in which the studio and all the people who depend on its output is the unruly factor.

Which is the anomaly—the orderly arrangement of his living space, or the chaotic state of his business affairs? Maybe neither. Are we not all made of contradictions, facets of cut stone that gleam with unexpected clarity when held up to the light, concealing the dark side? How can we decipher another when we do not know ourselves?

This yearning I have for Petro, for Auntie Safronia, for the simple times. What good is it? It leads me here, to this juncture, through all the things that happened. Nothing will change, no memory will be erased. No reason to believe anything better will come my way.

I go days without speaking to anyone, now suddenly I hunger for the touch of this man's hands, the wordless affirmation of a kiss. Hunger, sustenance: the poles of my blighted life. No matter how skillfully the repast is prepared, how generously shared, how satisfying its consumption—hunger returns. There is no healing, only moments of oblivion.

19

They walk side by side to the café. Serge describes some of the students in his art class. He's given them nicknames: there's Beethoven, with the unruly hair; *Maréchal*, who always wears his war medals and military cap; Babette, who can't stop talking about the generals she's known; Nature Lover—she only wants to paint trees.

Marfa laughs. "Is everyone who studies art so odd?"

"Not everyone. There are your usual earnest young students. But even they aren't exactly ordinary." They take a table outside, across from the entrance to the park, to enjoy the last of the sun's warmth. "There's one, I call him Alfredo—he actually wears a beret while painting. Like so." Serge folds his napkin into a square and perches it on his head at a rakish angle.

Marfa laughs again, covers her mouth with her hand. "But you like it, yes?"

"Oh, yes. I'm learning how much more there is to art than dabbing paint on canvas." He lifts his wineglass and sets it down again. "I'm sorry. I didn't mean... the work you do at Papa's studio..." He's tongue-tied, blushing.

She shakes her head. "We know what we do is not art. No one pretends otherwise, least of all your father." She sips her lemonade and blushes for her own reasons.

"Anyway, I'm grateful *Maman* agreed to pay for the class. I couldn't do it without her help."

"Tell me about your mother."

"*Maman*? She is lively, curious, loving. Generous. She has many friends. She likes to gossip and dance and go to the movies. She likes a glass of wine." He twirls his glass by the stem. "Maybe a little too much."

"What does she look like?"

"Petite, blonde, curvaceous. Isn't that what they say to avoid calling a woman plump?" He looks down at his own dimpled hands.

"You must resemble her."

"I'm taller, and my hair is darker, but yes, people say I do."

"How did she and your father—"

"I don't know the whole story. The way I heard it, they literally bumped into each other on the street. He knocked her off her feet. And the rest—"

Marfa smiles. "Yet they seem so different."

"They are complete opposites in every way. Maybe that's what intrigued them, why they needed to be together. And why they're now apart."

"There's no explaining attraction. Or love," Marfa says.

A crowd of school-aged children emerges from the park; they scatter in all directions, heading for home. The street fills with their calls and goodbyes. A group of boys stops on the corner, their voices raised in argument. They push and jab at each other, reaching for the soccer ball one holds just out of their grasp.

The one in the center, half a head taller than the others, brushes his hair out of his eyes and says, "Who scored the winning goal?"

"You did, Anatole," several boys respond in unison.

Anatole folds his arms across his chest. He looks confident, defiant, amused. He looks accustomed to winning, or at least getting his way. The boy with the ball hands it over. "So you get to take it home."

"Don't forget to bring it tomorrow," one of the others calls out, already walking away.

"Have I ever?" Anatole smirks, tosses the ball into the air, head-butts it toward the wall of the building. He sweeps up the rebound and tucks the ball under his arm. With a wave over his shoulder to the others, he saunters away. "Good game," he says. "See you tomorrow."

"Boys." Serge remarks. "It's all about politics, even at ten years old."

Marfa sits, hunched over, stiff, her hands clutched around the lemonade glass. Serge leans across the table and touches her arm. "Are you all right? You look upset."

"Oh, Serge." She seems close to tears. "Serge." She looks around at the other tables: a young couple deep in each other's eyes, a middle-aged woman with a book, three men in intense discussion punctuated with laughter, two teenage girls leafing through a magazine. "Can we walk in the park?"

20

It was inevitable that he would appear, not as the infant whose absent weight I will always feel in my arms, but as the boy he would have become—tall, smart, sandy-haired. Like his German father, with a touch more arrogance than he was entitled to.

As if I hadn't looked for him, in other women's baby carriages, among kindergarteners at the zoo, splashing at the water's edge at the duck pond, joyful and strange to me. No, not the water! I cried out once, pulling the child away, frightening him and his grandmother. How she glared at me. Crazy, she said. You're crazy, and rushed away, the boy too scared to cry.

I wasn't crazy. I knew he wasn't mine.

21

"I haven't been in this park in years," Serge says.

They walk through the iron gates together, then Marfa leads the way. "The lilacs are in bloom. Can you smell them? My auntie had two lilac bushes in front of our little house. What good are they? my father said once. You can't eat them." She's talking in a distracted way, head down, her feet scuffing at the pebbles on the path.

Serge puts his hands in his pockets. "What's on your mind, Marfa?"

"Let's go this way," she says. "There's a bench I like, under the willow."

They sit, not too close together, looking out at the deserted field, imagining the boys at their soccer game, running, shouting, falling, kicking.

"I had a son," Marfa begins, and stops. Serge waits.

"In Germany," she says.

"During the war?"

"Just before the end. 1945." She twists her hands in her lap.

"You don't have to tell me."

She looks up. "Yes. Yes, I do."

"What was his name?"

Marfa is silent for a long time. They sit stone-still. A squirrel bounds through the grass, leaps over their feet onto the trunk of a massive oak whose fledgling foliage casts its twilight shadows over one end of their bench. Serge turns his head; the squirrel clings, upside down, silvery tail pointing skyward against the tree's bark. Only its eyes move, darting glances at the immobile couple, assessing the danger level. An errant beam of setting sunlight picks up reddish highlights in its fur. They can see the staccato thumping of its agitated heart.

Marfa starts to speak, her voice tremulous, soft. Serge lowers his head, cocking an ear closer to hear her words.

"Everyone knew the war was ending. The lieutenant I worked for was gone. If he guessed I was carrying his child, he never said. While I worked for him I ate better than the ones in the camp, but I was thin, nothing showed until months later. I don't know what happened to him, if he ever got to see his family again."

"Did you love him?"

Marfa locks eyes with him, looks away. "He was never unkind." Serge doesn't know how to interpret this, but feels he shouldn't ask.

"The Nazis disbanded the women's labor camp. We were left on our own, without work or food or shelter, grasping at rumors. I joined my friend Galina and her mother. We traveled together."

"Galina who worked for us, along with her husband Filip? I remember them."

Marfa dips her head in agreement.

Serge frowns. "Weren't the Allies taking care of things, after the war? I heard they divided Germany into zones to restore order, resettle refugees."

"They did. The French, Russians, Americans, British all got a piece, set up DP camps and processing centers. That

took time, while we wandered like the beggars we were."
She pauses. "Our babies—my son and Galina's daughter—
were born in a German clinic near Regensburg. Then we
were back on the road, now with two infants and a few bun-
dled possessions. Some people, Germans, took pity on us,
gave us food or let us sleep in a barn. A few gave us milk
for the babies though they had little enough themselves.
Others chased us away like vermin. We traveled along the
river to keep a sense of direction. Though I don't know why
it mattered."

"Which river?"

"The Danube."

This time she is silent so long that Serge grows restless.
He picks up a handful of acorns, lobs them at random into
the grass along the path. Marfa looks out across the field.
She raises her head to follow a line of ducks flying toward
the pond behind the sloping hill. Her face is melancholy,
beyond sadness, her mouth clamped hard in what Serge can
only describe as longing. "Listen—" he starts to say.

The sun has nearly set, lighting the underside of clouds
in pinks and muted blues. A watchman leading a mongrel on
a leash tells them, "The park will close in twenty minutes."

They nod.

"Listen—" Serge repeats, and lays a hand on Marfa's
arm. She rests her hand on his, briefly, shakes her head as
if to clear it. Serge lifts his hand away, presses his palms
between his knees.

In a hoarse monotone, her eyes fixed to the ground, she
tells him about the endless rain, the constant hunger. About
sheltering under soaked blankets tented between trees.
About the refugees, all women and children, determined to

cross the river before daybreak at any cost.

"Why? What was on the other side?"

"The Americans. Someone had heard the Americans would not force Russians and Ukrainians to return to the Soviet Union, where we would surely die."

"Why? What had you done?"

"We had worked for the Nazi war effort. We were traitors, collaborators, in Stalin's eyes. We knew the French and British would send us back. But not the Americans."

She tells him how the women trudged for hours through riverbank mud, how some fell away, discouraged by the seething, rushing river. "But some of us went on. Galina's mother, Ksenia Simyonovna, is a forceful woman, determined and intelligent. She led us and we followed."

Marfa describes the bridge, the rain-swollen whirlpools just below its weathered planks, the way it swayed and sank into the water under their feet. "Ksenia Simyonovna tied Galina's baby onto Galina's back. She told me to do the same, but I refused. God help me, I chose this moment to stand up to her like a willful child, to announce my freedom from her domination. I simply couldn't let my son out of my sight. I refused. Do you understand?"

"I do," Serge says. "I often defy my father, even when I know he is right."

"Oh," Marfa seems startled at his words, the mention of his father. "Yes."

When she tells him how the women felt their way along the bridge in darkness, sinking waist-deep into the frigid water where the bomb damage was, clutching the rope railing with stiff fingers, too frightened even to pray, he drops his head into his hands. In the gathering dark, he doesn't see her weeping.

"The river took him." Her voice is dull, hollow. "The river took him, the current tore him, shawl and all, from my arms. I let go the rope, went after him, but the women pulled me back, forced me to finish the crossing while my baby drowned."

They see the watchman returning, the dog straining at the leash. They stand up and head toward the park gates. "I should have died," Marfa says. "They should have let me die."

In the intermittent lamplight, Serge looks pale, shaken. "No," he says. "No."

Back on the street she says, "His name was Tolik. Anatoly. It means sunrise. It was the end of May, like now. He would be ten years old, like those boys. Like Anatole."

22

Where were the tears then, when it happened, when any normal mother would have wept? Who needs them now? Now anyone would say, Ai, Marfa, it's in the past, it's no good crying. You're alive, aren't you?

Am I?

At least Serge didn't say anything stupid. Or anything at all. And that was fine. He looked so lost when we parted, I felt sorry to have burdened him with my tragedy.

I hadn't meant to tell him so much. It just came out, this boulder on my soul; there was no stopping it once it got rolling.

I didn't tell him all of it. I never will. How the next morning, when the sun came out, Galina wept for hours. Galina, pacing the riverbank with her child in her arms—her child, hungry and miserable but alive, in her arms. How I hated her, my only friend, with all my being, the rage burning in me, turning all love and grief and hope to ash.

The fear in her eyes when I took the wailing infant from her. Her face distorted with suffering, my suffering, mine, not hers, her swollen face wet with tears I could not summon.

What did she think I would do? Smash her child's head against a tree, fling her into the Danube, throttle her with my bare hands? Could I have done that? I'll never know.

My breasts ached with useless milk that mocked my vanished motherhood. I fed the child because she was hungry, because Galina's milk had run dry. Because I knew, ever since *those long-ago years of famine, what hunger was.*

23

"I thought you would not come." Meti steps aside to let her in. "Or maybe you misunderstood."

"I'm sorry," she says. "Is it too late? I had to—" But she can't think of a way to finish the sentence. Already, in the short walk from the park to Meti's door, her confession seems to have happened long ago, to someone else. Or to someone she used to be.

Still, something shows in her face, some trace of emotional upheaval she can't control. "What is it, Marfa? You look like someone's been chasing you. Sit down."

"Nothing. You're not angry?"

"Angry? No. Have you eaten?"

The rooms smell of lamb, rosemary, bay leaves. He serves her flatbread, ragout in a bowl, yogurt sauce in a teacup. She eats everything with such pleasure that she doesn't see him smiling until she's done. "You like my cooking."

She looks shamefaced, as if he's caught her out doing something forbidden. "It's so—" she searches for the word. "– intense. I don't know these spices. I grew up adding parsley to everything. And dill. Always dill." She frowns. "Even when everything else ran out, in the *Holodomor*, the famine, there was dill. It grew wild, needed no tending. The inspectors who came to take our livestock and empty our root cellars ignored it. But what good is it? You can't make bread from dill. For years after, I couldn't even look at it. The smell of it made me nauseous."

Meti nods. "I can imagine."

"Can you? Have you tasted soup made with nettles and dill? It's vile. But it kept us alive."

"What about pickles, though?" Meti looks pensive. "You can't make pickles without dill. Not good ones."

Marfa smiles. "That's what brought me back—my auntie's pickles. And later, learning German cooking in Bavaria. They like dill, too."

She stops talking. She looks lost in thought, her eyes clouded and distant. But the tension with which she arrived is gone.

Meti clears the table. They talk some more, about inconsequential things. Her shoulders gradually lose their stiffness, her face relaxes into the ordinary tiredness of a long day.

When she accepts the tea he offers, the brush of his hand on her fingers is electric.

Marfa is open, on fire. "Meti," she says. He meets her unexpected ardor, not wanting to know the reason for it.

24

What am I doing?

Meti's touch stirs me in ways long dead to me. Yet in my heart I feel nothing.

Do I still have a heart? Or did it spin away from me, concealed in the folds of my mother's shawl, in my failed effort to rescue my drowning child?

I'm left with flesh and blood, gratitude, desire without spirit or tenderness. Without life.

PART 2

1

The dress shop draws her like a magnet. Even when going through the Grand' Place is out of her way, she makes the long walk. Sometimes she moves past the window without stopping, catching the mannequin with a sideways glance as if afraid of her own reflection.

The dresses change every few days: yellow flowers on midnight blue, or pale green stripes bias cut to sway with every step. Once, a dazzle of scarlet silk, low-cut and sleeveless, made for champagne after dark. She barely glances at them; they are out of her reach, beyond imagining. These dresses are made for women in pretty shoes, to wear with a drape of scarf around the neck or a fur stole slung casually below the shoulder blades. Women she sometimes sees handing ribbon-tied packages to a waiting chauffeur.

What slows her steps is the hat—its black velvet simplicity, the rich extravagance of the curved green feather.

Marfa wants the hat.

This dismal afternoon, she stands before the window, her kerchief soaked through with relentless drizzle, and is startled to see a woman looking back at her through the rain-spattered glass. They are about the same age, the refugee and the shop assistant, slender, with the same springy reddish hair, though the dress shop woman tames hers with a pair of tortoise shell combs tucked into the wayward mass.

The square is nearly empty; a few intrepid passers-by

huddled under umbrellas dot the slick cobblestone plaza. The historic guild hall façades emit a dull glow through the mist. It's too cold to linger at outdoor café tables or stroll from shop to shop eating ice cream. This raw afternoon, the tourists are sheltering in restaurants or hotel rooms, or visiting museums.

The shop woman catches Marfa's eye, inclines her head toward the door. She doesn't smile, but her expression is welcoming. She holds the door open. "You might as well come in," she says. "No umbrella?"

"I left it home. The sun was out this morning." Marfa bares her head, shakes the excess water off her kerchief in the store's entryway, and hangs the kerchief carefully on the edge of the umbrella stand near the door.

The shop is smaller than she had expected. Half a dozen polished wood racks hold a few garments each. Scarves in floral or geometric patterns are threaded through a freestanding sculpture made of interlocking brass rings. Other accessories—a coiled belt, a scattering of silver bracelets, a pearl-handled brocade handbag—lie about on marble topped occasional tables, each caught in a circle of golden light from translucent porcelain lamps.

Marfa is aware of her cardigan's sagging elbows, her cotton stockings and scuffed shoes. She starts to back away, saying, "I must go —" but the woman is handing her a cup of steaming chocolate, the saucer balanced on a folded linen napkin. She leads her to a chair upholstered in red leather.

"Such weather," she says, sinking into the other chair. "No one will come today. I need someone to talk to." The woman sips her chocolate and closes her eyes. "This would be better with a little rum." She laughs. "I feel as if I know you. I often see you outside, looking." She laughs again, a quick burst that holds, as far as Marfa can tell, no ridicule or malice. "I am Odette."

Marfa can't echo the sentiment. She has never met anyone so glamorous, with such exquisite manicured hands. She swallows and murmurs, "Marfa."

Outside, a gust of wind worries the awning. The women watch rainwater stream from its corner into the clay planter beneath. "Is this your shop?" Marfa doesn't know what else to say to fill the silence.

Odette shakes her head. "Oh, no. I'm hired help. Madame owns everything. She designs the clothes and her two spinster cousins sew them in her atelier."

"That's why—" Marfa almost says, *there are so few of them*, but stops herself before the words slip out. "— that's why they are so unique."

"Yes. Lately, Madame has asked me to do some finishing. You know, hems, seams, buttons. But only in the back room, where the ladies can't see."

Marfa considers this, then takes a breath and says, "Why? I mean, why can't they see you working?" She blushes, realizing that selling the clothes, waiting on the rich customers, is also working, but shuts her mouth. Explaining will only make it worse.

"Oh, my dear. If they see me with a needle and thread, there will be no end to it. Can you put a few tucks here, to make me look fuller—" she rests a hand under her breast, then gestures toward her arm. "— or puff the sleeve to make it more playful? I tell you, there would be no end to it." She laughs, stands up and lifts the ceramic pot. "More?"

Marfa starts to refuse, then holds out her cup. *Why not?*

"But you," Odette says, sitting down, smoothing her skirt over her thighs. "What do you look at? What do you see? A special dress?"

"No. It's not the dresses I like." Marfa blushes deeper this time. She is inept at this kind of conversation, unbalanced by the chasm between this woman's life and her own gray existence. But strangely emboldened, too. Is it the chocolate, or Odette's open manner, talking to her as if they were equals? She runs the tip of her tongue surreptitiously along her gums, tastes the rich sweetness. "It's the hat," she says. "It never changes."

Odette studies the mannequin. "That's the strange thing about the selling business. Sometimes we have perfectly lovely things, and no one likes them." She shrugs. "Not enough to buy them, anyway."

"I like it," Marfa says softly.

"Do you?" Odette rises from her chair in a movement so graceful, so natural, it takes Marfa's breath away. "Try it on."

"No!" Panic grips Marfa's throat so she can barely speak. "I can't. I couldn't. My hair —" she meets Odette's eyes. "It's wet."

"Is it? Still? Let me see." Odette plucks lightly at Marfa's hair. "Only a little damp, on the ends." She shakes her own head, vigorously. "These curls of ours can be a nuisance, but they dry quickly, no?" She unfolds her pristine napkin and dabs at Marfa's head. "There. Now try it on."

Marfa takes the hat, caresses the velvet with her fingertips. "I've never..."

"Come to the mirror, here. No matter how much you like it, you never know until you try it on." She speaks with professional authority.

Marfa obeys. With both hands, she centers the hat just above her eyebrows, and frowns at her reflection.

"Farther back," Odette says. "On the crown. And tilt it a little, like so." She rearranges the hat so the feather curves toward Marfa's nape, gently fluffs Marfa's hair. She holds out the hatpin.

Seeing Marfa's hesitation, Odette pins the hat in place with a deft motion, without a word.

Marfa, too, is silent. She stares into the mirror, one hand raised to her mouth, the other over her heart. *Who is that?*

"You're a new woman," Odette smiles, reading her thought. "The right hat changes everything, it's the most important accessory a woman can have, along with pearls and a silk scarf. And this one, on you—look how the black sets off your hair, how the feather gives you style. A little mystery."

Marfa knows Odette has lapsed into her saleswoman's role, that she is practiced at finding the right words to flatter the customer. On a rougher scale, she's seen the same technique at work among aggressive flea market vendors. *The only one I have! Perfect for you!*

She does not care. She feels transformed, seeing her other self, the one she never knew she could be, for the first time. "Oh," she says. "But no, I..." She unpins the hat, holds it out to Odette. "The price... I can't."

"How much is it worth to feel beautiful? Anyway, the price I can fix, I will ask Madame. If you give me a little today, I can put it aside for you."

"You can? You will?" Marfa is wide-eyed. "But where will I wear it?"

"Anywhere you want, Marfa. A hat like this creates the

occasion. It gives you permission to shine."

On the walk home, the air is colder, the drizzle more penetrating. Marfa is bareheaded; in her excitement, she has left her damp kerchief in the shop and is too embarrassed to return for it. Leaving behind, also, an envelope, 'Marfa' written on it in Odette's fine script, the first installment on her purchase tucked inside. She calculates how much she will have to set aside each week and still have enough to cover her daily needs. She can do it, if she's careful.

And Meti? What would he think of her impulsiveness, her unexpected vanity? "He doesn't have to know," she says to the deserted street. "Not yet."

2

Style. Mystery. What do these words have to do with me? Meti says I am hard to know, my life closed even to his unquestioning affection. But style? No.

One dead child. Two. Grief. Failure. Disgust with the safety of acquiescence, choosing not to choose. A lamb to the slaughter. Even with you, Meti. Even with you.

What mystery? No one wants to hear about such things.

I want the hat.

You don't wear hats, he will say. So sure he understands this about me, when I don't understand it myself.

His touch fulfills me, but I'm afraid to yearn for it when we are not together. The alien firmness of his man's body, the way my fingers catch in the dense luxury of his chest. The peace, after. It all seems transient, not quite real. Each time could be the last.

The hat is useless, frivolous. I need good shoes, a new coat, a winter nightgown. I want the hat.

3

For the next several months, Marfa walks to the dress shop every Friday morning to pay her debt. She settles the next week's rent first, leaves herself enough money for food, essential supplies and trolley fare for bad weather days, and gives the rest to Odette.

It is a solemn transaction: each deposit in the envelope moves Marfa closer to owning the hat. Odette sweetens each visit with a treat—nougat or a bite of marzipan; if there is time before the first customers come in, a cup of tea.

One chilly morning when the square is slow to fill with pedestrians, Odette says, "Is there someone? Someone you will surprise with your new look?"

Marfa runs a hand through her hair and says nothing. Outside, a flower vendor arranges asters, zinnias, and chrysanthemums on a painted wooden cart. Gold, deep burgundy, pale pink and dusky blue blossoms brighten the autumn air.

Odette holds out a box of chocolates, does not repeat the question. She talks about her gendarme, who is married but comes to her when he can.

"He's good to me. Brings me little presents. He even likes my terrible cooking." Her laugh carries a sardonic edge, a hint of sadness.

"Does his wife know?"

"I expect so. Wouldn't you?"

They stand side by side gazing out the window. The flower seller stamps her feet against the cold. She rubs her hands together and tucks them into her armpits. She greets the first tourists to enter the Grand' Place with her sing-song: Flowers... Fresh flowers...

"It's a familiar story, as old as sex itself." Odette sighs. "An arrangement where each of us gets something we need."

Marfa takes a bonbon. She lets it melt on her tongue, takes a sip of tea. "Yes," she says. "I expect so."

4

This is foolishness. What am I doing?

Every time Odette puts my money in the envelope, I feel a little thrill at moving toward something new, something Odette says will change everything. There's fear, too: handing her the money feels final, as if we've started something that cannot be reversed.

Why is this hat so important? Am I ready to change everything? Maybe a few fresh flowers would have been enough.

Is there someone, she asked. Belgian women are so direct, they get right to what they want to know. I don't mind. I thought I would, but I don't.

I'm glad she let it go, didn't press me for an answer. I don't know what to say about Meti to anyone, least of all to myself.

I have known kindness. Auntie Safronia. Petro, in his way, too young to know how to be tender. Galina's friendship, and now Odette's. Meti, yes. Even the German never hurt me.

We each get something we need. Is that all? Is it that simple?

5

"I can't work here anymore, Meti." Marfa has waited until the others left for the break. She stands at his desk, holding her dinner pail in one hand. She looks determined.

Meti scans the last page of his newspaper before folding it in quarters. The movement reminds her of Serge, the day they laid the paint-spattered paper on the floor, the day they laughed and danced. By the time Meti looks up, the shadow that crossed her face at the memory is gone.

"Why not? You do good work." He stands up. "Have I touched you or said anything? Have I treated you differently? No one knows."

"Women always know," she says. "Don't ask me how. Maybe men, too, I can't say. But women know."

He shrugs, impatient. "Anyway, why do you care?"

"I care." After a moment she adds, "I can't explain why."

He lights a cigarette and walks to the window. "I like seeing you here, watching you paint. Remembering. Anticipating." He perches sideways on the sill. "It's only the job we're talking about, yes? Not—"

Marfa's face flushes red. "Yes," she whispers. "the job." Then louder, in a rush, "You'll find someone else to work, easily. Safya's oldest daughter is sixteen. One of the men has a nephew, just arrived from Morocco. Many people need work." She pauses. "I can't do it, *Patron*."

"*Patron*? Why so formal?" He turns to her just as Chantal

enters the room. Neither Marfa nor Meti had heard her approach.

"I forgot my money, for ice cream." Chantal, out of breath, stops in the doorway; her glance sweeps from one to the other, her lips twitch. She crosses the room, finds the change purse in the pocket of the sweater draped on the back of her chair, and is gone.

Meti coughs, blows smoke out the window. "Yes," he says. "I see." He sighs. "Go eat your dinner."

She shakes her head. She's no longer hungry.

"Walk around, then," he says. "No point giving them more gossip."

They both move toward the door and stop, separated by an arm's length of air thick with resonant silence. Marfa thrusts her chin out in a gesture that is firm and also somehow vulnerable. She meets his hooded eyes with clarity. It wouldn't take more than the lightest touch to break down the barrier between them. One kiss.

She steps toward the stairs. "What will you do?" Meti, behind her, has not moved.

"I can cook. Clean houses. Work in a factory. I'll get by."

"Stay through the week. Maybe I'll think of something." She's already in the corridor when she hears him say, "Come for supper."

The outside door opens just as she reaches the foot of the stairs. Serge, on the threshold, greets her with a radiant smile. Marfa grasps his shoulders with both hands and kisses him on the mouth. He is amazed, speechless. She brushes past him and runs out into the street.

6

Has anyone ever asked, Marfa, what do you want? What would I say?

Things happen. People decide, and I get carried along like a leaf on the tide.

The German was decent enough, and only that. I was important to him like having a tidy room was important, or a good meal served on time. A clean shirt. He could have had me anyway. What would I have done? But he chose to be decent, and I had no will to resist.

Tolik, he was mine. My sunrise.

Petro had my heart. He took it with him, tucked inside that Red Army uniform, the open greatcoat sweeping his heels as he marched away, singing.

My body remembers everything.

The nameless secret buried in the woods back home. I would have told Petro, but he was already gone. I wonder if he knows now, if they know each other, father and child. If names matter after you die.

What if it had lived? Grown into a child in whose eyes I could see my lover's smile, reminding me every day of what I had lost. And what had I lost? Petro could have become a drunken wife-beater, like so many others, his beauty and spirit twisted by the demands of a hard life.

I don't know what he thought, going off to war. Whether he took pride in his patriotic duty or simply relished the adventure, the relief from the drudgery of village work. We never talked about it. There was no time.

The letter his mother received didn't say if he fell at Moscow or Stalingrad, or perished in a field hospital, brought down by dysentery. A muddy trench or a roadside ditch. It said: for the glory of the Motherland.

And Serge? Who is he? Young, like Petro, his life full of possibility. Pure. No scars on his soul. Is he a shadow of impossible happiness, an ironic reminder of what will never be?

7

Marfa expects her last day at Meti's studio to pass like any other: work relieved with casual conversation, an uneventful midday meal. She intends to leave no canvas unfinished, her work space cleared of paint pots, cleaning cloths and brushes. She will simply go at day's end and not come back.

She is stunned when Safya, smiling, holds out the box tied with pink ribbon. Only Meti knows she has resigned; she has not told anyone else. She glances at him, accusing, but he's reading a book and doesn't see.

She sits speechless, the box on her knees.

The work table holds the remains of everyone's dinner. It's been raining since early morning and there is nowhere to go except a café. No one, not even Meti, considers going out. Only Serge, who attends a morning art class at the Lysée, is absent.

Beyond the open door, the men in cloth caps eat on the stairs, as is their habit. The taller of the two stands with his back against the wall, his dinner pail against his chest. The other sits on the top step with his water flask on the floor beside him, his meal in a bowl on his lap. They talk and sometimes laugh, but the room is too noisy for Marfa to hear what they are saying.

"Well, don't just sit there." Chantal tosses her fork into the handbasket at her feet and brings out a pear. "Go on. Open it." She rubs the pear on her sleeve before taking a bite.

Marfa's stiff fingers tug at the ribbon. She is unaccustomed to receiving gifts, especially like this, with everyone watching. The women gather around, the men in cloth caps occupy the doorway. Meti puts down his book, gets up from his desk and stands near the window, smoking.

"You didn't have to—" she falters. Her voice, tight and hoarse, catches in her throat.

"But we did. So open it, before *Patron* puts us back to work," one of the women says. Everyone, even Meti, laughs.

Marfa lifts the lid off the box and folds the tissue paper out of the way. She rests her hands a moment on the fine cloth inside, stares at the riotous flower design—phlox and buttercups, poppies and daisies and clover blossoms. Iris, moss roses, lily of the valley—all bloom in deep rich tones on a pale green ground.

"We thought you'd like the color," Safya says. "Maybe the flowers will remind you of your time here, painting with us."

Chantal puts the half-eaten pear on the table. She plucks the cloth out of the box and holds it at arm's length. "A green shawl goes with everything." She runs her fingers through the forest green silk fringe. "Here, try it on." She starts to drape the shawl around Marfa's shoulders.

Marfa recoils. Chantal steps back. "What's wrong? You sick?"

"I... no..." Marfa jumps up, lets the box slide off her lap onto the floor. "You should not—" She rushes from the room, head lowered. The men in cloth caps step aside to let her through. On the landing, she collides with Serge.

"Hey, what?" He steadies her, his hands on her arms.

"Marfa." He peers into her face. "What is it? You look awful."

"Oh, Serge. Serge." She leans against him, lets him hold her a moment before pulling away. "It's so beautiful. But I can't accept it. You know I can't."

"The shawl? The women thought of it. Every woman needs a shawl, they said. What's wrong with it?"

"Nothing. Everything. If it were anything but a shawl ... I can't accept it, Serge." She wipes at her face with both hands, trying to stop crying.

Serge looks bewildered. "You have to. They all put money in, even the men. And Papa and I helped. You can't insult them this way, even if you don't like it. Didn't your family teach you manners?"

He smiles and Marfa can't help but smile back.

She hesitates. "It would be rude, wouldn't it." She sighs. "All right, yes. You're right."

Back in the room, she picks the shawl up off the back of her chair and folds it into the box. "I'm sorry," she says softly. "You surprised me. Thank you." Her glance sweeps the circle of familiar faces. "You're very thoughtful." She looks at Safya. "The flowers, yes. They will always remind me of all of you."

"This damn rain," Meti says from his place at the window. "Hasn't let up all day."

They all pick up their brushes and return to work. Except for the afternoon concert of Strauss waltzes on the radio, the only sounds in the room are the creaking of chairs and occasional shuffling of feet on the worn floorboards. At the end of one worktable, Meti cuts new canvas into pre-measured sizes. He folds narrow cloth strips around the raw edges to prevent unraveling and keep the work square, secures the strips with glue. An hour passes. Another.

By five o'clock the sky is still burdened with storm clouds. The room feels damp and chilly. Marfa keeps her head down over her work, determined to finish the piece by day's end. Meti returns to his desk, picks up the book. Serge is sketching a hyacinth design, a gardening catalog open for reference on a corner of Meti's desk.

"What are you reading, Papa?"

Meti inserts his finger between the pages and holds up the book. "Yahya Kemal. A real poet. Shows you can honor the best of the Ottoman past while writing in the French style." He opens the book. "Listen:... oh eternally tormented sea," he reads in a musical cadence. "... in our souls we are one with you, in exile... no lovely shore would give rest to this agony..." He puts the book down, peers at Serge's drawing. "I hate hyacinths. They look wooden, artificial. Not like real flowers. And their scent makes me gag."

"I need more black, Serge," Chantal says. Serge gets up, retrieves a fresh container from the supply cabinet. "You know we don't like the same kind of poetry, Papa; yours is too formal or too sentimental for me. And I know how you feel about hyacinths. But people like them. We should do some."

"*Merci*," Chantal nods when he sets the paint down at her station. She is humming along with Michel Legrand's *I Love Paris* instrumental version, filling in the words in her throaty alto.

Marfa catches Serge's eye. "I like hyacinths," she ventures in a near-whisper. "They smell sweet." The glance he flashes in her direction, along with the briefest smile, is playfully conspiratorial.

Meti goes back to the window, perches on the sill. He tosses his cigarette out into the rain-soaked street, claps his hands, once. "Go home, everybody. This weather is too depressing. I'll pay you for the day," he adds, when several faces look up, questioning.

The workers gather their things, collect their pay, and begin to file out. Marfa is still painting. "Leave it," Chantal says. "I'll finish it on Monday." She buttons her raincoat and pulls a clear plastic rain bonnet over her hair. She smiles. "Good luck, Marfa. Think of us when you wear your shawl."

When everyone but Serge is gone, Marfa stands, awkward, at Meti's desk. "I didn't finish that one." She gestures over her shoulder.

"Never mind," he growls. "It's close enough." Their fingers brush against each other when he hands her the money for the week. He raises an eyebrow. She shrugs. "I don't know," she whispers so Serge won't hear. "Maybe."

Serge, in the doorway, rests one hand on the roll of butcher paper leaning against the wall. "We should change the table liner before you go." His grin is mischievous. He shakes his head. "I guess I'll have to do it myself. I'll miss you."

Marfa manages to smile. "Goodbye, Serge."

She picks up her dinner pail, holds the gift box tightly to her chest with both arms. She walks out of the room and makes her way slowly down the stairs, out of the building, into the rain.

8

There's a warmth about Safya I never sensed from any of the others. I wanted to say something to her. Not explain, no. There is no explaining about the wretched shawl that was to keep him safe, tied to me heart to heart. Ragged by then, moth-eaten, its brave red roses faded to almost gray, the golden foliage reduced to dirty yellow. Auntie Safronia saying, take this, it was your mother's. The soldier between us pushing the old woman aside. Schnell! Into the truck, Fraülein, and quickly!

Did they wrap me in my mother's homespun shawl, lay me down beside her while she slipped away, while her life oozed out onto the bloody sheets? Is that what happened? She died when you were born, Auntie Safronia told me, and nothing else. Was it so easy?

Oh, and he loved her, she said. Your father loved her.

What could I tell them, Safya, Chantal? How the river gropes me in my sleep, loosens the knots I trusted and rushes on, black and frigid. How it mocks me, trailing the cloth along the surface, the last thing I see before the whirlpool takes it all—my Tolik, my mother's shawl, my heart, my peace of mind. But not my life.

Serge said, I'll miss you.

What does that mean?

9

Odette has just brewed a pot of tea when Marfa bursts, breathless, into the shop. Marfa holds out the box, opens it. "It's my last day at the studio. They gave me this." She shakes her head, scattering rainwater like a drenched dog. "I don't know what to do."

"Don't you like it?" Odette holds the shawl up to the window. "Not to my taste, maybe, but beautifully made." She hands Marfa a tea towel. "Dry your hair. Take off your shoes." She strokes the shawl with knowing fingers. "Persian wool. Good colors. You'll be glad you have it if this winter's anything like the last one." She drapes it on a mannequin and steps back to admire it.

Marfa sinks into a chair. "It's not that. Of course I like it. But I can't … I can't…" She slips off her shoes and tucks her wet feet under the chair. The teacup Odette offers rattles against its saucer from the trembling in Marfa's hand.

"You can't what? I'm tired of hearing you say that. Do you know how much this cost? Think what those people had to sacrifice to buy it for you. What's wrong with you, Marfa?"

"Maybe they bought it at the flea market, in the Place du Jeu de Balles."

"Even so."

"I can't," Marfa repeats, stubborn. "It's a … a shawl." She lowers the teacup onto her lap and stares into it.

"Any fool can see that." Odette snorts. "And a fine one, too. Use it as a damn table cover, if you don't want to wear it." She looks exasperated. "You're making no sense at all today."

"Odette, please." Marfa looks up, her eyes clouded. "Take it, sell it. Don't ask me why,"

"Do you need money? Is that what this is about? Here—" She reaches for her handbag.

"No, no. You sell it, keep the money, or give it to Madame." She sets the cup down, still full, on the counter. She struggles to push her wet feet into her shapeless shoes and moves toward the door. "You're my only friend, Odette."

"I sometimes wonder why. You don't make it easy." She pulls the shawl off the mannequin and folds it with expert skill back into the box. "Take this. It's yours."

"No." Marfa backs away, opens the door and stumbles out into the street.

Odette follows her. They stand in the rain, arguing, the box like a weapon between them. "If you leave this here—" Odette's voice is firm, menacing. "– don't come back."

Marfa raises her face to the sky. Rainwater runs down her cheeks and soaks her clothes anew. She takes a step back, her foot slips on slick cobblestones and she nearly falls. Odette grasps her by the elbow and says, softer now, "Let it go, Marfa. Put your burden down."

They stand talking a long time, heedless of the rain, until Marfa takes the box. She crosses the square slowly, the sodden cardboard pressed to her chest. She doesn't see Odette drop her arms to her sides, her face a mask, her shoulders slumped in something like defeat.

10

Why did it have to rain today? So much, so long. Relentless. Dismal.

We stood in the downpour, Odette and I, arguing like two market women, she thrusting the box at me, saying, don't come back.

I told her, then.

Not everything. Not keeping house for the German, cooking his food, washing his socks, warming his bed. That story is as old as time, as war itself. It holds no revelation.

I told her about the crossing, the Americans on the other side. How on this blackest night Galina carried her baby on her back, and nothing happened to her. My Tolik was so small. If I tied him in a wet shawl over the wet clothes on my back, he would have been soaked through. He would have died of fever. At least on my chest I could warm him with my body. Didn't they understand that?

How can I let it go? I wrapped him in my love, tied him to me against the rain, the cold—and the river pulled him down by the only memento of my mother I had left.

No one said, you were careless, Marfa, it's your own fault. But we all knew.

It rained and rained, like today. It's still raining now. Meti sleeping, his arm around my waist, his breath on my shoulder. The shawl in the kitchen, hung over a chair to dry.

Odette said, Marfa, don't you see? This new shawl is not the grim metaphor for birth and death that you remember. It is not the emblem of your loss. It is life, friendship, hope. Rejoice in its colors. Accept the gift.

She could be right. My mind is too crowded with contradictions to work it out.

What is wrong with me? Why is kindness so stifling—Meti, Odette, Safya. Chantal, in her way, and the others. Even Serge. What do they see when they look at me? A refugee, a mouse content to nibble around the edges of what others leave behind. Will I ever be like others? Or are these kindnesses part of the punishment, a reminder that women who can't guard their children don't deserve a normal existence.

11

"Why can't you love me?" Meti lies on his back, looking at the ceiling. Light from the kitchen and the streetlamp outside the bedroom window make overlapping triangles on the carpeted floor.

Marfa turns on her side, facing him. She doesn't answer.

"Why?" he repeats. "We've been together now five, almost six months. Longer than I've been with any woman since... since I can remember. You come to me. You let me love you. But your mind is somewhere else. You're not really here with me."

She moves in closer, places a hand on his chest, her head against his shoulder. They pull the blanket up and sleep.

In the morning, Marfa boils eggs while Meti brews coffee. They move easily around each other in the small space, like dancers in a household ballet.

"You remind me of my father," she says. She salts her peeled egg and bites off the top.

"Oh?" Meti does not look pleased. "Were you close?"

Marfa shakes her head. "Not at all. It's the way you go after Serge, scold him all the time for no reason."

"It makes me crazy to see him wasting his life pursuing silly things instead of thinking about the future." Meti picks up his buttered bread and puts it down again. "So many opportunities have opened for young people since the war ended. How can he not see that? He's carefree now, his head full of nonsense, but what if he marries? With no education, he'll be taking menial work to feed his family, blaming fate for his own lack of ambition." He takes a big angry bite of bread. "Yes, I scold him, while his mother and his worthless friends — even you — encourage him behind my back. I scold him because I lost my youth fighting the Belgians' war. I scold him because I love him."

"That's the difference. My father did not love me. He criticized everything I did. Ordinary things, like washing dishes or sweeping the yard. He made me feel awkward and stupid."

"Do I do that to you?"

"Not to me, no. To Serge." She sets down her coffee cup and looks at him. "I feel good with you."

"Then —" Meti looks bewildered. "I don't understand."

"You resemble him. My father. You have the same open face, the same build. The impatience. And the resignation. When things don't go well for you, instead of looking for another solution, another way, you give up."

"That's not enough reason, Marfa. I'm not your father. You know that. And I don't give up when there's something I really want."

Marfa lowers her eyes. After some minutes, she stands. Her chair grates against the cracked linoleum floor. She picks up the breakfast dishes, pours hot water from the kettle into the basin, adds soap flakes. "On my seventh birthday," she says, "he came home drunk." Her back to Meti, she agitates the dish water with one hand, raising a trail of soap bubbles. "There was no celebration. Food was still scarce. We had no sugar, no butter, no eggs. Auntie Safronia had given me a pin, a swallow with outspread wings and a tiny garnet eye, a sprig of violets in its beak. She told me to hide it. I thought she meant, hide it from the government inspectors who came to take our wheat and vegetables and anything else they wanted to. No, my auntie said, don't let your father see it. It was your mother's."

She hears Meti shift in his seat and tap a cigarette from the pack on the table. The smell of sulfur hangs in the air, followed by the pungent aroma of Turkish tobacco, which she has come to like. "Do you still have it?"

"No." She half-turns. Meti sits in his chair, knees apart, squinting through the smoke, one hand resting on the worn twill of his trousers. He looks relaxed but also eager to be doing something: reading the newspaper, taking a walk. Marfa's eyes fill with unexpected tears. "I lost it in the... in Germany, in the crossing. I lost everything."

"The crossing?"

"Never mind. I don't want to talk about it." She returns to the dishes, her back straight, shoulders tense. "The only thing my father said to me that night, on my seventh birthday, was: why wasn't it you? Why didn't you die?"

"Instead of your mother?"

She nods. "She died when I was born. He never forgave me."

12

You're right. When we're together, I am often somewhere else, wandering among memories and ghosts. But I am also present. Is this what intoxication feels like? Everything sharp and blurred, here and far away all at once.

With Petro it was all one—the laughing and teasing, the dancing, the loving.

You, Meti. You take care of me. Feed me. Protect me like a child. I don't want to be your child. I don't need a father now.

After Tolik and the river, nothing. Galina's baby at my breast, that was animal instinct. The child was helpless, hungry. I had useless milk. On the farm, I had seen a sow accept a stray kitten, a cow adopt an orphaned calf.

And the other thing, that's animal too. Isn't it? The ache that rises in me to your need, stirred by your closeness, skin to skin. It also feeds me. I can't deny that. But it is not love.

It's glorious and sad, sad to the bone. Each time you ask to see me, I am surprised. When we part I feel like there will be no other meeting. You will get tired of waiting for the words I cannot say.

I love your son.

With Serge, I feel young, happy. Safe. He will never touch me the way you do, but he knows me in ways you never will. I trust him. He won't betray or hurt me.

13

Marfa takes the stairs slowly, not sure what she will find in the basement, what kind of work the handwritten sign on the building is offering. WORK AT HOME, NO EXPERIENCE.

"Piecework. Metal watchbands. Just as good as the expensive ones in the fancy jewelry shops," the man seated at the far end of the long room tells her. A single light bulb under a rusted metal lampshade hangs over his head. On the street side, three narrow horizontal windows near the ceiling are too dusty to let in any light.

He spills the contents of a cardboard box onto the table in front of him. The table's gouged surface is black with grime. His sallow face is scarred, pitted with smallpox; his sparse beard grows in patches, like clumps of winter grass. "It's easy. Look." He peers at her, frog-like, through thick cloudy eyeglasses. "Come closer! You can't see anything from over there. Sit down."

Holding an instrument the size of a dentist's pick, with a pointed end and a small wire hook near the tip, he picks up a minuscule spring and inserts it into the pre-drilled hole in the back of the band, anchors it in place with a deft twist of his fingers. "The band is perforated along both edges. Each hole needs its own spring. See?" With the tip of the tool, he picks up another spring from the jar lid he's using as a tray, and sets it in place. "Now you."

Marfa perches on the edge of her chair, trying to keep her weight off the broken rattan seat. The little spring she's targeted rolls and bounces around the tray, avoiding her timid stabs until she holds it still with her other hand and pushes it onto the instrument, pricking her finger. She gets it in place on the fourth try, feeling awkward under the man's gaze. He spits tobacco juice into a can, chews his mustache. "Try another one."

This one goes better, but not much. "I don't know if —"

"You'll get the hang of it," he interrupts. "When it's done, it looks like this." On the finished band he shows her, the diagonal segments align smoothly on the right side, crisscrossed on the back with springy ridges. He stretches and snaps it to demonstrate its flexibility. "It's modern and fashionable, doesn't rub or crack like leather. Stays shiny."

He looks at her, one furry eyebrow raised, names the pay rate. Marfa nods.

In a greasy cloth-covered ledger, he runs his hand down a fresh page to hold it flat. His thumb and two fingers look permanently stained a dull silvery-gray, the nails broken, dirty.

Under her name and address, he writes down the date and the number 500. "I pay by the hundred pieces. Cash. It shouldn't take you more than five minutes per band, with a little practice."

In a dark corner behind the table, he rummages for an empty shoe box, tosses in five prepacked sleeves of metal watchbands, a hooked instrument, and a bag of loose springs. "Come back when you're done, but don't take too long. I have a big order to fill."

14

People do this and call it work? I wish I had a paintbrush in my hand instead of this wretched instrument, so much like a dentist's pick that my teeth ache with every twist of the hook. When I complained about the monotony of filling rug canvas squares with color, I did not know what monotony was.

The ugly little man hidden in his underground room believes he's in the forefront of civilization, an agent for the changing times Serge talks about with such enthusiasm. Modern, the man said. Fashionable. He didn't say, made with the sweat of people like you, who will spend hours in deadening labor to avoid sleeping in the street.

I am not ungrateful. Because of this work I can keep my room, not have to count on Meti's good will for all my needs. If only the work wasn't so dirty. How long do I have before my fingers become stained like the little man's, the metallic grime ground into my skin?

Something else will come along. It always does.

15

"The café—you remember, in the snowstorm? They need a cook's assistant," Meti tells Marfa. "I told them you could do it." It's early morning, the sun just beginning to dispel the night's chill. He's walking her home.

"The Turkish one? With all those men? Why would they want me?" She sees again the man in shirtsleeves setting a plate of soup down on the table, then standing at the window looking out at the storm. The men smoking, reading, playing chess. Talking to each other over cups of tea in a language she does not understand.

"The owner's sister runs the kitchen. She's a hard-working woman. Not too talkative, and a great cook. You would be back there with her, not serving or chatting with customers."

"I'm sure they would rather have someone Turkish. What do I know about preparing your food?"

"You know how to chop and stir and garnish. I've watched you. The difference is in the seasoning, and you can learn that."

Marfa hugs the box of watchbands she had brought along to work on if there was time. After supper, Meti likes to scan the newspaper, or sometimes *Paris-Match*, reading interesting articles out loud, showing her pictures in the magazine. She can do a dozen or more bands before bed, earn a few more *sous* for milk or coal. "It seems strange,

Meti. I wouldn't fit in," she says now.

"Look, you need a job, don't you? Does your piecework even pay for your room?" He gestures at the shoebox in her hand. "Anyway, you could keep doing it for pocket money."

She knows it's true. The work is easy but repetitive, and the miserly pay is barely enough to cover her room and the price of coal, let alone food. Still, she hesitates. "Let me think about it."

"Think? What about?" He waves one hand in the air, exasperated. "They won't wait while you're thinking." Marfa glances at the watch on his upraised wrist. "Yes," he growls. "It's leather. I like leather. And the watch was my father's. He took it off a dead British gunner, after the Turks repelled the Allied attack on Gallipoli. Souvenir of 1915." He rubs his thumb over the watch face. "The only thing of value he ever owned, aside from his vegetable cart."

They walk in uneasy silence. At the entrance to her building, Meti stops and says, "Do you know what that... that operator does with your watchbands, why he works out of a filthy basement? He pairs them with cheap watches from Japan and sells them on street corners, in flea markets. Some people know they're imitations, but you would be surprised how many think they've found a real Swiss or German timepiece for a bargain." He's so worked up, he's actually huffing. "He can't afford a proper factory, so he takes advantage of desperate drudges like you who thank him for the opportunity to stay in poverty."

Marfa shifts the box to her left hand, opens the door into the hall with her right. She has seen the watch vendors, never gave them more than a passing glance or made a connection between their product and her labor. Alone in her room, she spends hours at her work, her table pushed up to the window to get maximum light. The odd little man had been right—she mastered the simple technique after the first twenty pieces and has settled into a steady if monotonous rhythm.

She misses the studio, the warmth and movement of people she had come to know, however slightly. Safya, gentle and strong, who might have become her friend; Chantal and her fresh mouth. The men in cloth caps, who shared nothing of their lives, whose names she never learned. She misses the radio, the day-long stream of songs about love and betrayal and sometimes, war. The smell of paint, glue, turpentine.

Serge, his energetic optimism and charm.

She knows every detail of Meti's two rooms, each object on his dresser, every dish and spoon and cook pot in the kitchen. She knows the slub and weave of his bedroom curtains, how the colors in the carpet change with approaching daylight. She cannot explain why being with him two, three times a week, while filling her with contentment, makes her feel even more keenly alone.

The prospect of spending time in a warm aromatic restaurant kitchen, even if she is only trusted to peel vegetables and wash dishes, is suddenly desirable. "All right," she says. "Tell them I'll come."

She has the door closed when she hears, "Papa? What are you doing here?"

"Taking a walk," Meti says. "What do you care, Serge? Time to go to work."

16

What are you doing here, Papa?

I keep hearing his question, its surprised tone.

And what is Serge doing here so early in the morning, on my street, in front of the building where I live? What does he know?

I am not ashamed.

The world has words for women like me, women who lie down with no resistance, who come when called. I offer no explanations. Least of all to you, Serge. I have nothing to say to you. I cannot justify my behavior even to myself. I can't face the condemnation I will see in your eyes.

What can you bring from your young, enchanted years that will help you understand? You have never lost anything. You know only love. Your only contact with the enemy in your country was taunting the retreating troops, shouting obscenities from the safety of a crowd of schoolboys. Isn't that what you told me? The war a game, your father's injury the only realistic detail when he came home to you, a hero of the Battle for Brussels. He scolds you out of fear born of disappointment. He knows how easily a life is shattered, wasted in spite of talent or intention. Life lived in imitation of desire because the moment for growth, for blooming, has passed.

I grow tired thinking about my life. Petro, my husband if only in my heart, keeper of my innocence. The German's hoarse whispers, spoken in darkness. Were they endearments, or veiled insults? No matter. He gave me Tolik, for a little while.

Meti, who is insistent, impatient, kind.

Where am I? I, Marfa.

I will do piecework, learn to cook Turkish food. Earn my daily bread. All to stay in place, every tomorrow like the day before.

Is this bad? Is there more?

17

She has not seen Serge since she stopped working at the studio. She remembers the day she kissed him, when she left him standing, speechless and bewildered by her impetuous act, in the vestibule of the studio building. Now he is there on her street, on the other side of the door, and she doesn't know why.

"I'll be there soon, Papa. After I stop for coffee," Serge calls out.

Meti says, "There's no café on this street." Marfa hears him walk away.

She starts up the stairs as quickly as she can, trying to make no sound. She knows Serge is still there, his hand on the doorknob; she can imagine the perplexed look on his face. The street door starts to open just as she reaches the second landing. She hears his rapid advancing steps, the tread familiar from all those days at the studio, his coming and going while she and the others worked.

Panicked, she ducks into the shared toilet under the stairs, leaving the door open a crack, not daring to breathe or turn on the light. Two floors above, Serge knocks on her door. She winces. "Not so loud," she whispers. "You'll wake the landlady."

"Marfa, it's me, Serge. Let me in," he says, then drops his voice as if he has received her telepathic warning. "I have news."

He knocks twice more. "Marfa. Marfa?" Then the sound of paper tearing, and after a moment, his slow, descending steps. Down the hall, she hears the slippered shuffle of a tenant heading for the WC. She slips the hook closure in place to lock the door, turns on the light.

"She must have gone out for breakfast," she hears Serge say in passing.

"I wouldn't know." The old man yanks on the doorknob, sending cold shivers up her spine. The little hook rattles against the brass eyelet, the metal shiny from years of rubbing one piece against the other. She pulls in on the doorknob, afraid the aged wood will surrender the flimsy lock to the man's urgent shaking. "Hurry up in there," he calls out, his voice both angry and pleading.

When she is sure Serge has left, she slips out and runs up to her room. Like an animal anxious to avoid confrontation, she is careful not to look the old man in the eye. "Women. A man could piss himself out here, waiting," he hisses.

The note under her door, scrawled on a page from the pocket sketch book Serge always carries, says:

> I'm going away. Meet me this evening at the
> French café near the park.
> S

18

I didn't go to the French café.

I went to the park. Walked around the pond. An old woman sat on the bench under the willow, a bag of bread crusts between her knees, her murmuring indistinguishable from the cooing of the pigeons around her feet. Our bench. My willow.

Going away. Where? Whether he is moving toward something desirable or leaving something dull or unpleasant behind, it's all the same to me. It means absence. No regrets.

I did not want to know about it.

From the stone seat near the park gates, deep in a horseshoe of lilac bushes, I heard the church clock strike six, then seven. The studio work day was done.

I saw him arrive. He sat at the corner table, the one barely covered by the restaurant's awning. Slanted rays of sunlight were there one moment, obscured by clouds the next. When he stirred his coffee, I thought I heard the sharp ping of his spoon against the cup. But no, that's impossible, from across the street, with streetcars and automobiles and people everywhere? You're dreaming, Marfa.

It started to rain. He turned his jacket collar up, moved his chair away from the dripping edge of the awning. Ordered another coffee, looked up and down the street. Waiting for me.

Why waiting? Why wasn't he running through the park, pacing the sidewalk, asking the waiter? Why not look up and see me? I was there, so close. Showered with damp lilac petals, overcome with their perfume: sweet scent, with a barely noticeable undertone of rot. He should be here with me, crushing me to his chest, our faces drenched with rain. Would we speak? Did we need to?

Ai, Marfa. Life is not a romantic Charles Boyer movie, with meaningful glances, passionate speeches and breathless silences. Serge was going away, his sights set on a future in which I played no part, taking my secret, my tragedy with him. Just as well. I recalled every word of his scribbled note. The word 'love' was not among them.

After another quarter hour, he stood, straightened his jacket, glanced in both directions like a child preparing to cross the street, and left. The rain, which had all along been only a drizzle, had stopped, evaporating into the evening air without a trace.

I didn't go to Meti's. Not that night, or the one after.

I went home.

19

Marfa imagines the café owner's sister to be ample, with soft arms and a ready smile for each of the men who comes for his daily dinner or evening pastry. She pictures a surrogate mother, kerchiefed, affectionate, ready to offer home remedies or sage advice for life.

She is not prepared for Fatma, who is tiny like Auntie Safronia. Kerchiefed, yes, but sallow-cheeked, and far younger than Marfa had expected. It's impossible to know whether a hard life or merely a sour disposition had etched the two deep furrows around her mouth. Marfa reminds herself that this woman, who looks to be in her mid-forties, has also lived through the war, either here in Brussels or somewhere else, in Europe or Turkey. The damn war. Has any woman come away from it whole, no matter what her age or allegiance?

"This is a bad time," Fatma says to her brother in heavily accented French. He is the shirt-sleeved man in the embroidered vest; Marfa remembers him from the night of the snowstorm, how he stood at the steamed-up window, looking out at the street. "What were you thinking, Selim, bringing her here at three o'clock?"

He waves a hand in the air, leaves the kitchen, then pokes his head back in. "She just came. She can sweep or wash dishes if you're too busy for her now. You said you needed help. What else do you want from me?"

"Someone who speaks my language," Fatma says under her breath—Turkish words Marfa understands only in their cold tone; annoyance requires no translation.

In French, she tells Marfa to start peeling potatoes, and fast—the men will be hungry. "When they come, we feed them. They should not wait."

Marfa fills two large roasting pans with washed potatoes, sliced under Fatma's watchful eye to precise specifications. "Like this, long wedges, then big chunks." The cook demonstrates with impatient movements of her quick thin fingers. Marfa sprinkles oil from a spouted canister, as directed. She stirs and tosses the chunks with her hands, following Fatma's pantomimed example.

She watches the cook extract a handful of spices and dried herbs from a clay jar at the back of the worktable and spread the aromatic mix evenly over both pans. "One hour." Fatma nods toward the oven spacious enough for Hansel or Gretel, or at least a whole lamb. "Then turn, stir. Twenty minutes—finish. Now soup."

Marfa smiles. Soup is familiar territory. Hadn't she and her auntie made soup every day of their lives together, even if only from nettles or dandelion greens and forest mushrooms? She knows about soup. Confidently, she moves toward the pot on the front burner and reaches for the knife to start chopping vegetables.

Fatma stops her. She needs to explain. Celery should be cut the size of her little finger, she says. Carrots to the first knuckle, parsnips quartered and sliced small. Onion minced and sauteed in butter, added at the end with a dollop of tomato paste. Marfa adds stock from a huge pot on the back burner, her ladle bumping against large hollow bones. The seasoning comes from glass jars with Turkish labels, yellow and greenish-brown powders she can't name, alongside pepper and salt.

"Get me some —" Fatma points to a row of herb containers on a shelf above the worktable. She seems to have lost the word. "Three or four big ones," she says, scowling. Bay leaves, Marfa guesses. They're the only big ones she can see. She holds out the leaves and says, "*Lavrovy list.*"

Maybe it's because Fatma reminds her so much of Autie Safronia, her small frame, her assurance, the particular way she wants things done. Maybe it's the tension of the last few weeks, not knowing how she would live on piecework, or how much Meti is willing to give or wait for. She had not spoken in her own language in such a long time, she is surprised when the words slip out of their own accord, sounding strange to her own ears.

"Oh." Fatma's eyes open wide. "You are Russian?"

"Ukrainian."

"Good. Now we talk better."

20

Meti says there were many Turkish people in Ukraine, especially in the Donetsk region, with its coal and salt mines. They came fleeing Ottoman oppression and stayed. Settled in so well that Stalin came to see them as a threat—loaded them onto cattle trucks and shipped them to the Caucasus and Uzbekistan, closer to the Turkish border for easy expulsion. 1944.

The year I worked for the German.

Whole villages were evacuated, families uprooted. Children who knew no other home forced to march on foot through the mountains to an unfamiliar destination. If they died, they died. History has no mercy.

What is Fatma's story? What pain, what indignity, what loss has she survived?

21

"Your mama teach you to cook?" Fatma scoops a quantity of flour into her wooden bowl, makes a well in the center with her fist. She adds yeast proofed with warm water and sugar, measures salt in the palm of her hand, drizzles in olive oil. When the dough is mixed and sticky, she turns it out onto the floured tabletop and begins to knead.

The question takes Marfa by surprise. Finding a common language has eased the atmosphere in the restaurant kitchen, even if in the last month all the two women seem to talk about is cooking and cleaning.

Marfa is grinding lamb for kebabs. She leans into the work, turning the wood-handled crank with one hand while feeding cubes of raw meat into the grinder with the other. "My mama died when I came. Auntie Safronia raised me, taught me everything."

Fatma looks up, says something sympathetic. Her hands continue to work the dough without stopping.

Marfa has watched Fatma bake the *pide* bread every day since starting work at the café. She is sure she can do it, but knows it's too soon to be trusted with this essential, almost ritualistic, task. Just as she knows that when it comes to seasoning the meat, she will do it under Fatma's watchful eye— how much sumac, cumin, pepper flakes, salt.

Fatma covers the dough with a towel, sets it aside to rise, and starts another batch. "You can run out of meat and the men will grumble," she tells Marfa. "But to run out of bread is unforgivable. Bread is hope."

Bread is hope. The words echo in the room.

Marfa cranks the grinder mechanically, her eyes fixed on a point at the far wall. She holds a handful of cool damp meat cubes above the feeding funnel. Pale pink bloody-looking liquid drips between her fingers onto the table.

"What is wrong with you today?" Fatma stops the grinder with a floury hand. "The machine doesn't know the difference between the meat and your hand. Pay attention!"

"I'm sorry, I was..." she doesn't finish the sentence, doesn't know how to talk about the jumble of images that flash like a silent film, stark and jerky, behind her eyes.

22

There's Auntie Safronia, sick. I watch her, the small thin body curved like a question mark under the bedding, her head low on her chest. I have never seen her face so pale, heard her breathe so—like a sweet old dog we had once when I was very little, who wheezed in its sleep until it grew quiet and still. No, I tell myself. She will get well. She must.

I stand at the foot of the bed, making no sound, willing her to open her eyes. And then she does. She looks at me and smiles. "Marfa," she says. "How are you?"

The question is so strange, I don't know what to say. I'm not the one who's sick! I giggle.

I bring her chamomile tea and some dry bread crusts. She sits up, takes the cup with both hands, inhales the healing steam. I dip the bread into the tea and hold it up to her mouth. She eats slowly, with pleasure. When the cup is empty, she sighs. "Let's read," she says.

There's her old metal bed, just wide enough for two of us. I settle in next to her, feel the heat of her receding fever, and place Krylov's Fables on her lap. I've already finished reading them in school, last year in first grade, but Auntie Safronia has only read two—about the fox who wanted grapes, and the rooster who liked corn better than precious stones. I don't mind reading them again, and we both like the animal pictures: lambs, oxen, wolves, bears, and many kinds of birds, some of them in coats and fancy hats.

"You start," she says, but soon she takes the book from my hands, holds it up close to her face, and reads it herself. Her voice wavers a little, sounding out the syllables of longer words.

I feel happy and proud. When she has finished the story, I say, "Tell me again about why you never went to school."

"Again? All right, come under the blanket."

Outside, a drenching rain beats against the ground. It streams in sheets down the windows. A night wind shudders the panes. Why does the wind sound so ominous after dark?

Am I afraid? No. The animals are fed. There's bread in the pantry, and jam, too, and kasha with fried onions on the stove. The firewood is dry. Auntie Safronia is feeling better, and tomorrow there will be sunshine.

She lies back on the pillow. I snuggle into the circle of her arm and listen.

I was the middle child, the third daughter. By the time I turned six, there where four more: two boys, two girls. My mother, worn out by farm work and childbearing, could not manage so many by herself. With my father away on the railroad for weeks at a time, and likely to have spent much of his pay by the time he came home, she was left with no one but us children to share the daily tasks and run the little grocery store in the front room.

The older ones, the first and second son, were enrolled in the village school and went on to attend *gymnasium* in Kostroma, where my uncle was postmaster. My big sisters, too, finished the village school, where their education stopped. "Who will marry them, after all that schooling?" my father said. "They know enough to keep household accounts."

"You had to be seven to start school, right? Just like now," I

break in.

Auntie Safronia nods.

I had shadowed my older brothers and sisters since I could remember, listening while they read their lessons out loud, intrigued with the mystery of writing in blue notebooks. I counted the days to my birthday, expecting to be transformed overnight into a schoolgirl with a pinafore and book satchel. I would wear shoes every day. I would sit at the table with the others after supper, reading and writing.

There was no pinafore, no satchel for my birthday; only a pair of red silky ribbons for my braids.

"You must have been sad," I say

"Why don't you tell the story? You've heard it enough times. I'm tired."

"No, Auntie. I like to hear you tell it." I stroke her hand, the skin rough and dry to my fingers. She sighs again.

All right, I thought. It's summer. Mama is busy with the new baby. Soon, before school starts, she will make me a pinafore. I had been helping with the little ones since I was five. Maybe if I did more, tried harder, she could rest a little and have time to sew.

I tried. I washed their diapers, fed them and played with them, keeping them out of Mama's way so she could run the store. Would anyone notice?

"They noticed," I answer, and Auntie smiles.

Me, seven years old, holding baby Ivan—your father— on my hip while stirring the soup. Later, when he slept, I showed little Sonya how to feed the chickens. "Good girl," Papa said, and I glowed. I went to bed happy, sure that now Mama would sew my pinafore. Soon I would start school. Soon.

From my bed, I heard them in the kitchen.

"What do you want from me?" Papa sounded irritated. "I can't stay here and bake the bread or clean the house for you. I won't."

"From you? I want no more babies." My mother's voice, low as it was, carried clearly up to the sleeping loft I shared with the younger children. My older sisters stayed in town during the week with our aunt, who was a teacher. One worked in a cake bakery as a cashier; the other was a tailor's assistant. The brothers, now fifteen and sixteen, shared a room behind the store.

Mama coughed, long and hard. "I need a woman to help me with the work."

"A woman. Anything else, Madam? A new gown for the Emperor's winter ball?"

My mother's chair scraped across the floor. I heard her moving around the room. The large pot we used for boiling laundry clanged against the stove. She was angry, that was clear. Was she also crying, the way I did when things went wrong and I didn't get what I wanted and couldn't stop the tears no matter how hard I tried?

"I know what that's like," I interject. "I hate crying, but sometimes I just can't help it." This time, Auntie lays her hand over mine.

After a few minutes, Papa said, his voice softer now, without that sarcastic edge, "Anyway, you have Safronia. She's small but quick. She can help you. And the little ones adore her."

My breath caught in my throat. I pressed both hands over my mouth to keep from making a sound, and hung my head over the edge of the bed so I wouldn't miss anything.

"Safronia?" My mother lifted the pot and crashed it down on the stove. "She needs to go to school."

"What for? To learn how to cook kasha? We sent the older girls. Now we see them only on Sundays, with their city manners and no husbands on the horizon. Women don't need book learning."

I heard Mama lift the bucket we kept near the door and pour water into the wash pot. "Is that what you think?"

"Yes. What do you know? You don't travel the country or read the newspapers. You don't know what's going on in the cities, where students and foreigners are stirring things up, talking about revolution. Safronia can learn to sign her name, like you. We'll teach her how to use the abacus, so she can run the shop. She'll be useful and stay out of trouble. I have decided. Safronia stays home."

"Oh." The empty bucket hit the floor and rolled away. "You have decided. And tomorrow you leave. Who do you think decides things when you're not here? This stupid, uneducated woman." She coughed again, the spasms so sharp I thought I could feel the pain in my own chest. She slammed the bucket on the floor. "Get me some more water from the pump."

My father laughed. "Exactly. You manage perfectly well. Education doesn't make you smarter, it makes you restless." He went out, leaving the door to swing open against the wall, creaky hinges whining. The night air carried the rustle of leaves from our apple tree into the room.

"How did you feel, Auntie?"

"I felt—I don't know how to describe it. Hot and cold, furious and so, so disappointed. As if my life had ended right there on that night. As if nothing good would ever happen for me

again. It wasn't my father's decision that made me lose all hope. It was his laughter."

"Then how did you learn to read?"

"Marfa." She cups my chin and raises my head to look at her. "You know that part very well."

"I like to hear you tell it," I repeat.

My brother Silvestr taught me the alphabet. He was the oldest. He liked me. When he was home, he helped me carry water or bring in firewood, and he talked to me in a serious way. He gave me his old school notebooks so I could trace the letters and start to read.

Auntie Safronia pulls the blanket up around our necks. The room grows chilly, but neither of us wants to get up to feed the stove. "You know," she says, "brothers and sisters don't always get along in a large family. I was lucky to have him."

"What happened to him?"

He was a student at the Kyiv Police Academy. A cadet. He wanted to be a detective, come home and serve our village and the surrounding area, help people, uphold the law. When the Bolsheviks came, they demanded every cadet sign an oath to support their revolution. He refused, and they shot him, right there in the school yard, for all to see.

We grow quiet, Auntie and I. When I look up at her, her eyes are closed, but I know she's not sleeping. "You never told me that, about the shooting," I say in a small voice. "Only about how he helped you learn the letters."

"You were too young. Maybe you still are."

"I'm eight," I remind her. "Almost nine."

"I know." She pauses. "Anyway, that's what happened. Those were terrible, terrifying times. You couldn't trust anybody." She opens her eyes and gives me a long look. "You still can't. Don't

ever say a word of this to anyone, Marfa. Ever. You hear?"

I promise. But she need not worry. I have no one to tell.

I don't like school, but I have to go. It's the law.

The boys, noisy and sure of themselves, seem to take up all the air in class. Except tall, quiet Petro, who never pinches or pushes like the others, who likes to sing. When I stand next to him during the singing that starts and ends each day, his clear strong voice carries me. I lift my head a little higher, sing a little louder. Petro is my friend.

And no one else. The girls are talkative and cold. I hate the way they gossip together in groups. What do they have to talk about?

They have mothers, those girls. I love Auntie Safronia with all my heart, and know she loves me. How would having a mother be different? I can't guess and don't care. Why does it seem to matter to everyone else?

And fathers. Mine isn't the only one to leave for a construction job on the Dnieper dam. Many men go, leaving their parents and families to work the land. Not all of them disappear, like mine. That short, bowlegged, freckle-faced girl with snake eyes and a sharp tongue—what is her name? She carries letters from her father in the pocket of her pinafore and brags about the parcels of cloth and boxes of chocolate he sends home. "He's a work inspector," she tells anyone who will listen. "A leader of the people."

Surely some of the fathers also come home drunk, and say ugly spiteful things that lodge in your mind, your heart, making you feel like nothing, less than nothing. Surely mine is not the only one. I know I should love him; I do not. I'm glad he's gone.

In school, we keep our opinions to ourselves. We chant patriotic Soviet slogans under the kindly gaze of Lenin surrounded by smiling children, on the wall—but I know better than to repeat them at home. Is it instinct, or the unspoken disapproval on Auntie Safronia's face, the fleeting frown, the tense set of her mouth? The way she always finds something else to talk about—have you swept the yard, or, bring in the laundry, Marfa, it feels like rain. Or, let's read.

Let's read. The first time Auntie says those words to me I'm sure she is joking. I'm not happy to be in school. Doesn't she know that? I like the farm, the cottage, the river, the sun. She is not joking. Now that the worst of Stalin's hunger years, our Ukraine's deadly Holodomor, is over, she wants, finally to learn properly to read.

Holodomor. 1932. The dreadful time. Sometimes, walking to the meadow for nettles or dandelions, or, if we're lucky, wild mushrooms, we see people lying beside the road. Dead people. Some of them are missing an arm or a leg, their sleeves and pants torn away, caked with blood. No shoes. Auntie Safronia tries to block them from my sight. She moves between us, saying, see that cloud over there? It looks just like a horse. She talks about the berries we might find at the edge of the woods.

But I do see. That woman from our village crouched in the weeds, a hatchet in her hand, her dress hanging in dirty folds over her dry stick of a body. Is it a log she clutches, wrapped in that bloody rag? It's not a log, or a baby, either. Logs don't have long blue fingers.

The time Auntie covers my eyes with her hand: too late. I see the naked body face down in the mud, large raw wounds where its buttocks should be. "Stupid birds," I shout, while a pair of crows pick at the corpse, ignoring my waving arms. "Who are these dead people, Auntie? Why don't their families bury them in the cemetery?"

She doesn't answer. I guess she doesn't hear me.

She says to me, over our supper of bitter greens, "If anyone offers you meat, or stew, don't eat it. Run away."

"Why?" It's been weeks since we caught a rabbit—a little one. I can barely remember how it tasted. Why would anyone turn down food? Who would be willing to share any?

"It could be bad meat. It will make you sick." She averts her eyes, won't look at me. It's not like her. She always speaks plain to me, teaching, explaining.

"Why, Auntie?" I ask again.

"Why, why." She is angry. "Just don't eat it, I said. Even if you're hungry."

I'm always hungry. There's no need to say it.

And this: the famine is in the past, the war with Germany has not begun. Me in the yard feeding the chickens. We're poor, like everyone else, but not without hope. The crops are in, the inspectors no longer poke their noses in our pantries and cellars looking for hidden food supplies. Through the open door I smell the Sunday supper Auntie Safronia is cooking for us, meat and vegetables and roasted potatoes.

Feeding the chickens—I love how the grain flows through my fingers like water; how the hens crowd each other to claim the best kitchen scraps. How they keep a wary eye on the rooster who can, at any time, take whatever he wants. Their heavy bodies balanced on slender legs, their smooth heads bobbing up and down, pecking, pecking.

Hens. No, crows. Lustrous feathers blacker than the blackest sin, big sharp beaks tearing human flesh. Auntie Safronia's cold tight voice saying, don't eat it, run away. I see again the woman with the ghoulish parcel under her arm, running like a thief even though no one is chasing her. I understand the horrible secret no one talks about, the desperation fueled by starvation fever that transforms ordinary people into savages.

My arm freezes in midair, the grain rains down on the hapless chickens' heads, "My God," I whisper. "My God."

23

Marfa stops grinding, covers her mouth with the hand that is slick with meat juice from the lamb, realizing she has said the last words out loud. "My God," she repeats.

When Fatma looks up, her eyes hold a question tinged with concern. "You were far away," she says, her voice mild. "Finish the meat. We can have coffee while the dough rises."

"How did you come to be in Brussels?" Marfa wraps her hand around the little coffee cup. Her fingers, stiff from cranking the grinder, relax in the smooth porcelain's warmth. She knows that being the first to ask a question is a good way to deflect attention from herself. She would rather ask than answer just now; listen, not talk.

Selim pokes his head in the door. "What do you need from the market, Fatma?"

Fatma jumps up, hands him the list she's been keeping on a nail over the work table. "Why do you speak to me in French?"

"So you will learn it better." He scans the list. "Eggs, dried apricots, prunes, bulgur, mint, lemons, eggplant... I could send Marfa."

"No. I need her here. Just go, before we get busy."

Selim lowers his voice, but Marfa, standing near the back window, can still hear every word. "She's working out well, yes? I thought so. A hard worker."

Fatma lapses into a torrent of Turkish. Selim raises a

finger. "French. Speak French," he scolds. "Anyway, she would be a good wife, even if she is thin and homely. There's a heat under that modest exterior."

"Heat? What heat? Don't talk nonsense."

"Any man will tell you. Meti would be a fool to let her go."

"You're the fool, Selim." Fatma shakes her head, laughing. "Don't meddle. Just go." She turns to Marfa, still smiling. "Brothers," she says, and adds something in Turkish that Marfa can't understand.

She tells Marfa how to season the meat and form it into kebabs ready for grilling, and turns her attention to the bread dough. With a chef's knife, she quarters each ball of dough and shapes the pieces into long flat rectangular loaves. "Brussels," she says. "It's a long story." She presses the back of the knife down the length of each loaf, in two strips several centimeters apart, leaving a perforated trail along which to tear the finished bread. "Hand me that cloth, to cover the bread. Yes, the embroidered one. It was my grandmother's."

The cloth is stained, showing the evidence of many years' use in the thinning weave of vintage linen. Marfa admires the vibrant needlework along its edges, stylized floral patterns in red and russet adorning delicate scrolled vines, tender leaves. "It came with me through all the journeys, from Ukraine to Belarus and Poland, to Germany and finally here. It's a long story," she says again, and Marfa knows it can't be a happy one. She knows she will not hear it today.

After the loaves have risen, Fatma brushes each lightly with olive oil and adds a sprinkle of black sesame seeds.

"Check the oven, Marfa. Make sure it's hot enough."

24

The bread, baking, smells divine.

Bread is hope, Fatma said.

All those years ago. No bread at all, every scrap of grain impounded by the inspectors. For the Motherland. For us, no bread at all. Where was hope? Are we dead yet? Is this hell?

In the labor camp, the Germans gave us bread with sawdust. Hope with fear. Illness, death. Our bellies hard, bowels knotted or suddenly loosened, stinking of shame. And then, the war is over. This camp is closed, they said. Go. Where?

There is the Danube, black, indifferent. Me sheltering under sopping blankets with Galina, the only friend of the heart I've ever had. Feeding our babies. Our hope. Swallowing moldy bread when we can get it, and grateful for it.

Looking for the Americans. They will help us, people said. Did they? Yes. DP camps, real food, wholesome bread. Piles of clothing to choose from, enough for everyone. Take! We never stopped to think where it came from, not until much much later. Who wore this dress, these trousers, this child's coat? Where are they now? We only knew Americans have everything.

Getting there, across the wretched river, the price was too high. Unspeakable. The ransom: give up the only thing you love, Marfa, and with it faith, and joy, and hope.

Tolik, I couldn't keep you safe. I didn't know how. Is there life without hope? Yes. Yes there is. But no amount of bread will make it bearable.

25

Marfa doesn't know how to ask Meti about Serge. She can't say, he came and left a note in my room. When she overheard their chance meeting outside her door, it was Meti who sounded uncomfortable, defensive. She must wait, hoping he will tell her where Serge has gone, and why. If Serge is angry with her for failing to meet him at the French café, she may never know.

They don't go out together much, she and Meti, except for an occasional walk in the park. She would like to go to the cinema, or the Grand' Place, stroll among the market vendors, watch the lace makers at work, admire the sweet artistry on display in the chocolatier's window.

She would like to show him the hat she admired in the dress shop.

Greta Garbo might wear such a hat—black velvet, the green feather curving back around the brimless edge, sophisticated in its simplicity. She can feel the way it will hug her head, held in place with a pearl-tipped hatpin, once she has finished paying Odette for it. "You don't wear hats," she can almost hear him say, and it is true. What would she answer?

They go on as before, except Meti has stopped leaving notes at her residence; he drops in at the restaurant kitchen for his daily coffee. He brews his own cup, takes a pastry from the tray near the door. "Hello, Fatma, Marfa," he always says. "All is well?"

Marfa looks up from whatever she's doing. If he raises an eyebrow, she either nods or frowns. She no longer blushes at their secret code: *Come, tonight.* Is it really a secret? Or does everyone guess, like the women at the rug studio, with their knowing glances, their silent scorn?

At the café, the women only leave the kitchen to use the WC. Selim takes the orders and serves the food when Fatma rings the bell to tell him it is ready. Through the briefly open door, Marfa can see the men, who sit in groups, talking, smoking. Like the night of the snowstorm, some play chess or read books and newspapers. There are never any women.

What must they have thought of her when Meti brought her in, wet, bedraggled, shaking with cold? What kind of woman did they think she was? Yes, that kind. And why not? Why not. Even though back then there was nothing between them.

Now, this day, Meti stands inside the door, baklava raised to his mouth, honey dripping from his fingers. "Give him a plate," Fatma says, "and wipe the floor. No ants in my kitchen."

Maybe it's something about Marfa stooped at his feet, mopping the sticky drips with a wet rag, something about the way he stands over her, watching. Maybe Fatma has caught the signal that passed between them. When he's gone, she says, "He's a fine man, Meti. You know he was hurt in the war?"

Marfa doesn't dare answer. She turns away to hide the hot flush that starts on her neck and mottles her face. She's seen the scars, her finger has traced the pattern of raised flesh mapped on his thigh. She bends her head to her task, peeling onions for the day's stew.

Fatma spoons tea leaves into a blue ceramic teapot, fills it with boiling water. Marfa inhales. The clean, bitter aroma takes her into a place of comfort, a desire for the universal pleasure of a cup of tea. "Is there a nation on earth where people don't drink some kind of tea? I can't think of one," she says, surprising herself with the remark, relieved when Fatma seems not to have heard it.

"He gave us money to open the restaurant." Fatma centers the brewed tea over a larger matching pot filled with hot water and places both on a filigreed copper tray, next to an ornate cup filled with sugar cubes. "I was a widow with two children. My brother and me, we had nothing but a wish, an idea. A Turkish gathering place to make our men feel at home after the war. Meti raised the money we needed to start, and helped us with the authorities." She places four tulip-shaped glasses on the tray and rings the bell for Selim. "He can have all the baklava he wants."

26

Those men who come every day to the café. They must have families. Wives, children. Parents. How do they live? Why is it so important to spend hours in the company of other men, every day?

I don't know what Meti does the nights we are not together. If he has another life, filled with friends or music, men and women who laugh and sing. Though if he liked those things— laughing and singing—wouldn't I know it? Or does he reach for the poetry shelf near the bed, his hand choosing a book at random, to read until sleep takes him. Getting up to undress, turn off the light. Yes, that seems more likely.

That day he told me he had been to the Natural Sciences Museum to see the mammoth skeleton and the world-famous sea shell collection: I would have liked that, I said. I wanted to say, can we go? But I have never been able to ask for anything.

Sometimes I think he's ashamed to be seen with me. Because I'm not Turkish? Because Turkish men don't walk with their women in public? That is not, cannot be true. His Belgian wife was not one to endure being hidden away. Maybe that's why they are estranged.

Maybe we all want more than any one person can give us.

The night of the snowstorm was different; he probably saved my life. No one thought, in that moment, about propriety. Did they? And we had not begun, then.

Or had we? I feel as though there was always something

between us, before touching, before the kitchen, the bed. The food we cook and eat, the flavors in our mouths—tomatoes, garlic, mint, sweet onions—sensual as a kiss.

No one, no man, could be more attentive. Why can't you love me, he says.

Why can't I? What is deficient in me, that he can reach me in my most intimate places without touching my heart? I am pierced with desire, yet I do not love him. The flaw is clearly in my own character. It's not enough to say, the war. Didn't countless women experience abuse, suffer hunger, know terror? I know how to stay alive; I just don't know how to live.

The one I love is the one I cannot have.

Serge. It does no good to tell myself he's just a boy, not much older than Petro was all those years ago. It's an infatuation, Marfa. What the romance magazines call a mirage of the heart. Knowing that doesn't change anything.

I could not meet him at the café, spying on him instead like a silly girl. Did I believe that if I did not talk to him, he would not go? Now he's gone, and I don't know where or why.

27

"I've had a letter from Serge," Meti says.

Marfa picks up their plates and turns to face the wash-basin, her back to the table. What can she say? I didn't know he was away? Does he ask about me? It's the first time his name has come up since she failed to keep the café rendez-vous, weeks ago.

"From Serge," she echoes his words over her shoulder, not trusting her voice, afraid to reveal the turmoil his words have caused.

"Sit down." Meti lights a cigarette, exhales. "The dishes can wait. Do you understand how surprising this is? I never expected to hear from him until he came home."

"I'll just make the coffee," she says. She watches her own hands with detachment, spooning coffee, sugar, reaching for the spice jar on the shelf. By the time the water boils, she has calmed down a little. "When will that be?"

"What?"

"That he comes home."

"Summer holidays, I expect, same as other schools. Why should art school be different?"

Art school. "I thought you disapproved of art school," she ventures, her tone cautious, neutral. She remembers the fierce arguments, Meti's enraged reaction to any mention of Serge's art studies.

"I do. It's a way for families to save face among their

friends, pretending that their dilettante offspring are engaged in something meaningful." He watches Marfa sprinkle cardamom into the cups and fill them with coffee, her movements graceful, competent. "I like the way you do that," he says. "Your brew is always perfect."

"Fatma taught me." She looks at him, then drops her gaze. "Thank you." She can't suppress a little smile of pleasure at the compliment. "But —"

Meti stirs his coffee with the tiny spoon. "And the other ones, the starving ones, their lives fixed to some higher purpose. Sponging off so-called patrons while they —" he paints the air with an invisible brush "— develop their talent. They really annoy me. As if there's anything noble about being poor."

Marfa sits down. "But Meti, the studio, the rugs. Why do it if you think art is useless?"

"Pure chance. I was starving, waiting for the veteran's pension to start, with a wife and child to support. When I found the roll of canvas, I couldn't ignore the opportunity. I copied the first designs from my sister's carpet, found others in books and magazines. I was amazed when people bought them, with the war just over." He lights another cigarette.

"Still." Marfa knows she's treading on shaky ground, but curiosity compels her to pursue the thought. "It takes a certain skill, a natural aptitude, doesn't it? To make art, even if it's not original." She sets her cup down carefully on its saucer.

"Art," he snorts. "That's not art. Anyone with a steady hand, a little dexterity can do it. Even you." Marfa flinches at the implied insult, but Meti does not notice. "Those people—Chantal and the others—you think they do it because it's art? They do it because it's easier than working in a factory. They do it for money." He gestures for more coffee, sips, smokes. "What Serge is doing has nothing to do with money. How will he live? Ask him."

Marfa shakes the coffee grounds into the waste bucket and submerges the cups and spoons in the washbasin's lukewarm suds. "Then why did you let him go?"

"I did not let him. He went against my wishes. His mother paid."

Marfa washes up, empties the washbasin in the WC down the hall from Meti's rooms. The table is clear of everything but his cigarettes and the single red carnation he brought her the day before, still fresh in a water glass, and Serge's letter.

She sits down. "What does he say?"

28

I can picture his room. I hear the delight when he describes the little table with one short leg, the eaves above his window where pigeons roost at night or shelter from the rain. The thin lumpy mattress. Good thing Maman sent him a warm blanket!

There he is walking around Liège, buying pommes frites from a street vendor for his midday meal, and later maybe some beer. The oil and salt cling to his fingers; he wipes them on his pocket handkerchief (I know he has one, he doesn't need to say it.) He says he's studying the city's architecture with freshly observant eyes, noticing line and form and ornament as never before.

I smile at his portrait of Mme. Silvanot, who smokes a pipe and talks incessantly, though she demands near perfect silence from her six boarders: four male students and two aging spinsters. She's a war widow. What would women like Mme Silvanot do without such employment? How would they live? What would Belgium's cities and towns be like without these guardians of morality, civility, and thrift?

Meti cannot keep the sarcasm out of his voice, yet I feel Serge in the room, his energy, his soft animated face. I feel his happiness, and wait for the words I know must be coming.

What would we have said, that night at the café? Me hiding like the coward I am, what words was I afraid I would not hear? Or worse, words I could not speak without reducing myself to the caricature of a woman who sleeps with one man and loves another.

When Meti sighs, folds the letter and tucks it into its enve-lope, my heart sinks.

Serge does not ask about me.

29

"Did you love your wife, Meti?"

Marfa doesn't know what compels her to ask such an intimate question. She is relieved when he does not answer right away; she half-hopes he did not hear her.

"I was fourteen when my father died. I became the only man in a houseful of women," he says at last.

They are walking in the park. It's Sunday afternoon. Lilies bloom in lush display along the gravel path, their golden heads sway in unison, one way then the other, obeying the midsummer breeze.

There is something about the act of walking that encourages conversation. Random thoughts surface, thoughts she might otherwise suppress, contemplate in silence, or dismiss. It was on such a walk in this very park, months ago, with Serge, that something prompted her to reveal her life's catastrophe, the drowning she thought she had buried forever. She has not told Meti about Tolik, about the wind and rain, the tiny hand glowing against black water. Her mother's shawl. She knows she will not talk about it now.

Meti walks with his hands folded behind his back, *like a poet or a philosopher*, she thinks, and smiles at the comparison. It's not altogether untrue. For all his bluster, she knows he is contemplative, a reader of poetry. She has lately realized she likes both sides: the crusty taskmaster and the thinker.

"Do you know what it's like to become the family decision maker when you are still a child yourself? When you know these women—my mother, my aunts, my older sisters—know better than you do what needs to be done, and only defer to your half-formed opinion out of cultural custom. To make you a man." He shakes his head. "Except my grandmother," he laughs. "She took no nonsense, taught me to treat women with respect, reminded me to stay in school, and to think before I spoke. I haven't been altogether successful at that—thinking before I speak."

Marfa takes one hand out of the pocket of her sundress and reaches up to push some wayward curls out of her eyes. "How did it feel? Did you like taking charge?"

"My father was a forceful man, virile and proud; a solid example of a man's place in the family. I guess I learned from him in spite of myself. But I knew the women had the wisdom and experience to decide where to live or how to handle bureaucracy. Soon enough, though, what started as a courtesy to my male status became a habit, for all of us. Especially after the war. When I started the rug painting venture, I had no trouble convincing my mother and aunts to do the early work, evenings, at the kitchen table. No argument, even though they had little spare time."

They walk in silence part way around the pond, where water birds begin to gather in noisy groups, squabbling for space, preparing for nightfall. Marfa's original question hangs in the air, unanswered.

"What drew you to her, your wife?" she ventures, with a quaver in her voice.

"Oh, well, you know I've lived in Belgium since I was small. I had Belgian friends—not many, but enough to get a taste for a non-Turkish point of view. I was a Belgian citizen. I served in the army, took a Nazi bullet for my country. It's the immigrant dilemma, balancing between the pull of heritage and the reality of your surroundings. You know about that, maybe, more than I do."

"Yes," she says. "Though I was taken from home by force. It's not the same."

"Hmm."

They stop under a stand of tall old pines. Marfa studies the rough bark blooming with gray-green moss, the trunks dotted with knots, like syncopated eyes on a ceremonial mask. She will not ask again.

"Your question," Meti says. They resume walking, heading around the pond's far side toward the north gate. "Annette—who likes to be called Annie—was lively and curious, not bound by strict rules of acceptable behavior. She used nail polish and lipstick. She wore her hair short. I was beguiled by the back of her neck, her lovely exposed ears. I was dazzled." He pauses to glance at Marfa, who keeps her head lowered, eyes on the path, and does not see. "And she liked me. Some say another person's admiration is the catalyst to love."

"Do you believe it?"

"I think so. Yes."

"What happened?" Marfa's voice is barely a whisper.

"Her friends. Some of them mocked me for failing to keep up with them, for not drinking or dancing. She became impatient with me, dissatisfied." He pauses. "And infidelity. That also happened."

30

Another person's admiration is the catalyst to love.

Is that true? Do we find it easier to love those who admire us, and they, by virtue of their admiration, slip into deeper feelings for us? Is that what happens?

There may be some logic to this idea, if there is any logic when it comes to love.

And the other thing, the desire. The need for touching, being touched. It lives apart from yearnings of the heart but is it all of a piece, all one in its mysterious way?

The German did not love me. It's not enough to admire a well-pressed shirt or a perfectly broiled cutlet. Yet he was gentle with me and practiced in seduction. He found the place in me I hadn't known anyone could reach. Loneliness is an aphrodisiac, too, it seems. On both sides.

Does Serge admire me? When I think of him, I see his boyish enthusiasm, his optimism. His self-absorption. Does he think of me now in his new life away from home, steeped in his studies? He must be angry I ignored his note and failed to meet him. He must think I don't care.

What do I want from him? I don't know.

What happens to love when admiration ceases or leads to disillusionment?

The question I did not ask was: do you still love your wife, Meti? And also, whose infidelity?

Because I don't know if love can die. Maybe the heart simply grows bigger, makes room for new loves among the previous ones.

Meti admires me. He says so. He loves me. He says that, too.

I am touched by his affection, at ease in his company, surprised by his forbearance. Aroused by his presence. Will his admiration kindle love for him in me? Is it inevitable?

Is being dazzled the same as love? Am I dazzled by Serge?

31

When Marfa thinks of the watchband man, whose name she knows but prefers not to say, even to herself, she feels a chill, a cloud. She has gone to drop off the finished work early, before going to the café. She can take half the money to pay down her debt to Odette, and still have enough for her room, if she takes an extra hundred bands and finishes them by Friday.

In the evening, Meti grumbles over the time she spends at her monotonous task. The dishes are put away, and he has read all the papers, French and Turkish. "Will you be long?"

"Not long. I just need to finish these." She looks up. "It's a warm night. You could take a walk, buy cigarettes."

"I don't need cigarettes, or a walk," he snaps. "Why do you have to do this, anyway?"

"To pay for my —" she almost says *hat*. She bites her lip, twists a pair of tiny springs into the band on the table before finishing the sentence. "— my room."

"Why do you need that hole of a room? You could live here, with me. I've told you."

She shakes her head, does not answer. Works faster.

Meti goes down the hall to the WC, returns, puts away his towel and soap. Marfa hears him move around the bedroom, the familiar sounds of his undressing, the creak of the bed springs under his weight. She hears him strike a match, smells the tang of sulfur and the sweet smoke of his cigarette.

She tries to keep working, but her hand trembles; wire springs spill from their tray and roll across the table. Her head aches, her eyes hurt.

Meti turns out the light and says, "Come. Now."

32

Marfa scrubs her hands daily with laundry soap after working on the watchbands. Especially the right, which has begun to show a pale gray shadow where her hand rubs against the metal. It bothers her; she does not want to carry a metallic tinge on her fingers or have the residue find its way into the food she handles. She does not want to exhibit the permanent stain of this occupation on her skin, like the watchband man.

The soap is harsh. It puckers her hands until they look like chicken skin. Fatma shows her how to smooth away the dryness by massaging in a few drops of warm cooking oil.

Marfa is folding Meti's laundry, while he reads aloud from a *Paris-Match* article about Marilyn Monroe and her new husband, Arthur Miller. When he pauses to turn the page, she says, "Give me this handkerchief, will you?" She holds up a blue plaid one, the lines so faded they appear translucent, a hole the size of a hazelnut in one corner.

He looks up, surprised. "Of course, but why? If you need a handkerchief, I'll buy you a new one."

"No, I prefer this one," she says. She goes to the bedroom, puts away his things. She likes the intimacy of handling the shirts and socks and underwear he has entrusted to her care. Neither of them thinks of it as payment for the food he provides—it's part of their shared life, the natural balance between them.

When she returns to the table, he picks up the magazine. "All right, if that's what you want." She ignores the look of faint amusement on his face.

Marfa unfolds the handkerchief and lays it flat on the table. Meti stops reading. He watches her fold the cloth over her right hand and pencil a rough outline, avoiding the hole. She cuts two pieces in the shape of a mitten. "Go on with the story," she says. "I'm listening."

In Meti's utility box she finds—among safety pins, loose shirt buttons, mismatched shoe laces, candle ends—a needle and thread. While he reads, her hand moves deftly around the shape, leaving a trail of small neat stitches. Within minutes, she bites off the thread, turns the mitten right side out, and slips her hand inside.

"I don't understand," he says.

"To keep my hand clean while I work. See?" Marfa twists half a dozen springs into a watchband, her cloth-covered hand resting against the unpolished metal.

"Wouldn't a glove be better?"

"Too much trouble to sew. I use only two fingers to do the work, but the underside of my hand gets dirty. I don't want to smell like a tin can, either." She puts her tool away in the watchband shoe box, lays the mitten inside and closes the lid.

"Women are so clever," Meti says. "I never would have thought of that."

Marfa takes up the magazine. "Have you finished the article? Let me see the pictures."

33

Is Marilyn Monroe happy?

She looks carefree, the way she throws her head back, laughing, flirting, her neck and shoulders bare.

I see the beauty when I look at her.

I don't see much joy.

Sometimes, her eyes are guarded. Sometimes they hold the sadness of too much adoration, a hint of crushing loneliness.

I know that look.

34

Odette laughs when Marfa asks for the glove. "You're not serious. What will you do with one opera glove? Do you like opera?"

"No. I mean, I don't know about opera. What will *you* do with it?"

"I could display it with a diamond bracelet or a pair of rings, in the showcase." She turns it over, passes it from hand to hand. "Though it would look odd, by itself. And I have no one-armed customers just now." She looks up, catches Marfa's eye. "Take it," she says.

"Will Madame —"

"No, she won't miss it. I found it in the scrap cloth basket, near the bottom. And look, it's stained, besides." Odette points to a greenish spot on the palm. "The only thing it's good for now is dusting the furniture. Is that why you want it? To dust the furniture?"

"Huh," Marfa scoffs. "You haven't seen my furniture. This glove, is it silk? It would slither away and hide rather than touch my things." She wiggles her hand in the air, laughs.

Odette studies her friend, her expression sympathetic. "It's peau de soie, yes. Silk. From Italy." She presses the glove to her cheek, then holds it out to Marfa. "Put it on."

"What? No, Odette. I've just come from the kitchen, my hands smell of lamb fat and garlic. And these clothes..." she looks down at her flowered skirt and dingy blouse.

Odette slides to the edge of her chair, her face aglow with irresistible enthusiasm. "Never mind all that. I want to see it on you. Put it on, put it on."

All at once, Marfa can picture her friend as a girl of twelve or thirteen, trying on her mother's cabaret shoes, a string of beads draped around her neck, wishing she were bold enough to paint her nails or use the curling iron. Playing dress-up: something she, Marfa, in the perpetual poverty of her village existence, would never think to dream of.

She slips her hand into the glove, and stops. Odette drops to her knees, pushes Marfa's sleeve up out of the way and smooths the pearly cloth between Marfa's fingers and over her arm, stretching it into place above her elbow. Odette stands up, steps back. Marfa holds her arm away from her body, elbow bent, fingers extended, as if it doesn't belong to her, as if it's something fragile, easily broken with one careless movement.

The women look at the glove, then at each other.

"Oh," Marfa says. She strokes the satiny fabric with her free hand. "It's so ... rich." She starts to peel the glove down her arm, inside out. "How do I take it off?"

"Loosen the fingers." Odette looks serious, plucks at her own hand to demonstrate. "Then slide it off."

"Thank you." Marfa looks up. The glove lies loosely now across her knees. "Are you sure it's all right?"

Odette smiles. "I'm sure."

35

I couldn't tell Odette why I wanted the glove. How I would cut it off at the wrist to replace the handkerchief mitten, so flimsy it didn't last more than a week. How I would use the excess cloth to dust Meti's furniture. She doesn't know about the watchbands, or the pathetic worm of a man and his basement hideout.

How did he come to be like that? What series of disappointments led him to this subterranean existence? His toad skin and greasy hair make him ugly but not altogether repulsive, downtrodden but not defeated; I have lived among worse human specimens in the labor camps.

His enterprise must be more successful than it seems. I have seen packages on his table addressed to shops in Charleroi, Tournai, Malmedy, Namur. Does he advertise in the newspapers? I can't imagine him traveling to show samples of his product to anyone, but I suspect he is not as poor as he looks.

Why was I surprised when he assaulted me? Why should his underground life make him different from other men? And how swiftly he moved—in his chair one moment, then one hand on my neck, the other gripping my breast, my back pinned to the wall.

It must have been the nauseating stench of his tobacco-stained mustache, the metallic grime of his filthy little hands, that stirred the rage in me. For the first time, I said no. Leave me alone. And pushed him. Where was that strength before?

I know the answer, don't I. He's no seducer, no sweet-talking lover of women. I met his force with mine, his urgent demand with my resistance. Any woman would. Wouldn't she?

I suppose men can't help themselves when it comes to women. What a burden that must be, to live like cats on the prowl, always alert to possibility, ready to pounce and stun, drop and run at the first sign of trouble. Well, maybe not all men; many do cherish their children and are devoted to their work. The Turkish men—I feel them looking at me when I come in, or walk to the WC from the café kitchen, even though not one has ever approached me or said a rude word. I feel safe. Still, it's there, the appraisal, in their eyes.

But to slam the box of bands down on the table and head for the staircase out of there, that felt good. Him calling out, please don't go, you are my best worker. Forgive me.

If I walked away, how could I finish paying Odette for the hat? Ask Meti for the money? Never.

I feel a little sorry for him, the toad, now. I didn't then, struggling to breathe, choked with too much anger to be afraid. At least he did not offer me more money, as what? Compensation for his beastly behavior, or complicity, silence. That would have been the end, hat or no hat. Take his guilt-induced charity? Better to be in debt to my landlady, or skip the tram and walk to work every day.

He couldn't meet my eyes. Imagine. A man who can't look Marfa in the eye. Forgive me, he said again, when I picked up the box of new work and left.

Forgive me. Words no one has ever said to me.

36

"This hat," Odette says, "will change your life." She has opened a bottle of the champagne she keeps in the back room for the best customers.

Marfa smiles. It has taken months to reach this moment, months in which the seasons changed, the air became cold and warm again, snow turned to rain, and flowers bloomed. She raises her glass, following Odette's movements, the way she's seen it done in the cinema, those afternoons when she is free from work.

Meti went with her once, and spoiled the event with his restlessness, his incessant scornful mumbling. "Let's go," she said at last, annoyed.

He seemed surprised. "It's not over. Don't you want to see the end?"

"I have a headache. Let's go."

"What do you like about that film?" Meti asked later. She remembers him sitting on the bed, watching her change her workday dress for a faded nightgown. "It's ridiculous. Wouldn't you rather be here, like this?" He pulled back the blanket.

She hadn't answered, not at once. When he turned out the light, she said, "When I was little, my auntie told me fairy tales. Everyone who was idle was either stupid or evil, and beauty was the same as virtue. This American film, this new fairy tale where being rich is no crime—I like it. Even if it is ridiculous."

She went back to the theater alone a day or two later, in the afternoon, to see the end. No, real women didn't dress like that, and what kind of man spent his life in evening clothes and dressing gowns? Meti was right. But they were lovely, these make-believe people, the ladies in their gowns and high-heeled slippers, with perfectly waved hair and stylish hats. The men in silky smoking jackets—did anyone actually wear those?—who needed the help of a valet to put on a bowtie.

She sank into their world, in the dark theater. What was it like to lounge in bed against a cloud of pillows, picking with manicured fingers at the contents of a breakfast tray, scanning the daily paper, folded by a well-trained servant to the social pages? Even if no one lived like this, not even in America.

She doesn't like the champagne. It tastes sour, like fruity vinegar. *Sec*—a strange dry word to use for something poured from a bottle. After reading about it in novels, watching its nonchalant consumption on the film screen, she finds it gaseous, with a bitter aftertaste. Too polite to dampen her friend's pleasure, and mindful of the expense, she takes small dutiful sips and tries not to let her distaste show on her face.

She shouldn't have worried. Odette is too absorbed in her own cause for celebration to notice Marfa's reaction. She sets her glass down and picks up the hat, runs a finger along the length of the feather. "I've dressed many women here, working for Madame. Of course, I fret about their appearance, try to make them look their best, even if they don't follow my advice and insist on wearing things that don't flatter them—too tight on the hips, or the wrong color. But you know the truth? I don't really care. Let them wear what they want." She lowers the hat to her lap and gazes out the window.

Marfa is surprised to learn that Odette may be unhappy. "Why do you do it, then? What would you rather do?"

"Hah. I can't sing, like my mother. I can't even cook, like you. I'd rather be here waiting on the rich than changing bedpans at the hospital, or teaching spoiled children geography. Here I get nice clothes, and sometimes my gendarme takes me dancing. What woman do you know who does what she wants?"

Marfa thinks a moment, says. "Madame? Though I don't know her."

"Yes, Madame. In exchange for the comforts of a home life, a family. She and those spinster cousins. It's sad. A sad life."

"She must have friends, for the theater, the opera. Lovers."

"Ah, lovers, of course. And how long does that last? She is past fifty now. Who will look at her in ten, twenty years, and see beyond her success, her eccentricity? Who will know the woman, and love her?"

"Why not?" Marfa says, almost to herself. "Things happen..." Her head feels hollow. She could tell Odette now about the puzzle of her life, the thing that is not happiness but is not much trouble, either. About Meti. If only Odette would ask.

It is the hour when the daytime crowds have gone and the evening strollers have not yet appeared. Two or three flower vendors, sturdy-looking country women in rough clothing and wooden shoes, the last participants in the day's market, pack up their tubs and baskets and wheel their carts toward the streets leading out of the square.

Marfa watches, too. She wonders about their lives, about the hard work needed to provide such an ephemeral product. Is there joy in it? Is there more than commercial satisfaction in handing an armful of flowers to a customer, flowers that both seller and buyer know will fade and die before morning? Or are their minds too full of worry about hungry children, aging parents, perpetual debt, to see the beauty?

"This hat," she hears Odette repeat, and turns her attention back to the room. "The day you came in. Do you remember? You were cold and wet and a little—I don't know—lost."

"You gave me chocolate. It was hot, comforting. A treat." Marfa feels obliged to sip from her glass, swallows without wincing.

Odette dismisses the compliment with an airy wave. "That was nothing, the chocolate."

No, it was everything, Marfa thinks.

"But the hat. The way your eyes lit up when you tried it on. Your head a little higher, your shoulders straight. I doubt you noticed it yourself."

A young woman comes in, glances at Marfa. Frowns. "Ah, Mademoiselle," Odette says, rising to meet her. "Will you join us in a glass? Your jacket is ready."

Marfa retreats to the back room. The wine glass seems alien, unnatural in her hand. She sets it down on Odette's worktable, wipes her moist hand down the side of her dress. From her vantage point just inside the doorway, she can see the young woman in front of the mirror.

"I shortened the sleeves, took a tuck in the back," Odette says. "It fits you perfectly." Her tone is businesslike but also, Marfa notices, subservient, without the lilt, the ease she slips into when the two of them are together.

"It's so severe," the woman whines, and accepts more champagne.

Odette lifts a brooch from the satin-lined tray on the counter, something delicate and ornate in silver filigree. She pins it to the jacket's lapel. "Yes," the woman says. "That will do. You may add it to my bill." She leaves with her purchases without showing the least sign of pleasure, no thanks for the service or the refreshment.

Odette seems unaffected by her customer's patronizing treatment. She locks the door, turns out the overhead light, and joins Marfa in the workroom. "Drink up," she says. "I can't save this for tomorrow." She brings out a small dish of wild strawberries. "I got these from a fruit vendor this morning."

The champagne tastes better, Marfa finds, its acidic edge softened by the sweet berry juice on her tongue. She drains her glass, does not refuse another. Somewhere beyond the rushing in her ears, she hears Odette's voice but can't make out the words.

She stares at the row of thread cones on a low shelf behind the table, watches the colors blend into each other and out again. White, pale green, yellow, electric blue, several shades of red, black. The space is cluttered with dressmaking tools: pincushions and chalk, cutting shears and little scissors for snipping seams. An ironing board, and, near the coal stove in the corner, several sizes of flatirons. The tailor's form wears a tape measure around its neck; with a flourish, Odette places the hat onto the headless manne-quin and steps back smiling.

Marfa laughs. *No arms, no legs, no head.* She laughs and laughs, hard and loud, in great throaty spasms until her shoulders shake and her face is wet with tears. "Marfa," Odette says. "Marfa —"

"It's the war. Don't you see? With one hand, the war gave me a child, and then took him away with the other." She talks rapidly, as if afraid she'll run out of breath, or time. "The war that turns ordinary people into unfeeling mon-sters. That burns all the decency out of your soul and scars everything it touches. That kills the capacity for love."

She weeps, long and silently, until Odette brings a towel from the washroom, wipes her face and makes her blow her nose, drawing a reluctant smile.

"Oh, my dear." Odette takes her hands. "I know you've been through terrible things, yes? You don't have to tell me again." She pauses. "Maybe it was the war, and maybe not. People capable of cruelty will find you and hurt you. They don't need war to do it."

"Maybe you're right. It was my own fault. My obstinate stupidity," Marfa pulls her hands away to wipe at fresh tears. "And now, when there is something good, and I can't ... I can't..." The crying subsides into shuddering sighs.

After a long silent moment, Odette says, "I've told you my mother was a cabaret singer. A beautiful woman. She used to say, when someone gives you something—a gift, or a compliment—with an open heart, say thank you and accept it. When it's your turn to give, you'll know." She holds out the hat. "Put it on."

And Marfa does.

"You know, I would have given it to you, or charged much less. But Madame is not generous; she keeps strict accounts."

"I would not have accepted, Odette. How could I? I'm sure you understand."

"Look at you. This makes me very happy." Odette smiles broadly and empties the last of the wine into their glasses.

Marfa turns her head from side to side, admiring her reflection. She arranges her hair with her fingers, letting the russet tendrils curl here and there over the hat's black velvet edge, until she is pleased with the effect in spite of her blotched cheeks and puffy eyes.

She makes her way slowly across the Grand' Place, weaving a bit among the couples and families out for an evening promenade. Her head is spinning; she doesn't care if she looks like a chambermaid trying on her employer's finery when she should be sweeping the parlor, if the hat on her head bears no relation to her plain dress and shabby shoes. The empty hatbox Odette has given her swings from her fingers when she stoops to pick up a pair of moss roses fallen from a merchant's cart or someone's purchased bouquet. The frilled blossoms are nearly white, with deep blushing centers. The stems, covered with downy flexible thorns, prickle agreeably against her skin. At the corner, Marfa dips her hand into the lion's mouth fountain and drinks from her cupped palm, giggles when water runs down her chin, soaking her collar.

She will not see Meti tonight. She will go home, eat her baguette, sit at the window and watch the sky fade, the moon rise. She will place the roses on the windowsill, in an empty jam jar she has somehow kept for just this purpose, for these orphaned flowers that, while lost, have escaped being trampled into the cobblestones.

The hat will rest on its hatbox, behind her, next to the hairbrush on her dresser. She doesn't have to look at it. She will know it is there.

37

Say thank you, and accept it, Odette said. Take it. Good advice, I'm sure.

She has been—is—my friend. Am I her friend?

She has lived her entire life in her own country, among her own people. What do I know about her kind of dissatisfaction? She conceals it under that sophisticated exterior, the smooth surface that gives nothing away. Some people hide behind the flow of words, while others crouch in silence, like me. We each find our own way to move through the days, and the nights. Only she is lively and sociable and I am merely odd.

Raised by a cabaret singer. Was it glamorous, exotic? Or lonely for a child, a life with dangers and pitfalls, at the mercy of men in dinner jackets, musicians passing through. Entertaining the occupation troops, German officers. The other side of the Hollywood fairy tale, where women have few defenses. What can an adolescent do? Nothing. I know, don't I?

What do you know about that world, Marfa, about the glitter tinged with seediness? Is desperation more bearable when dressed in an evening gown, accompanied with music? Stop weaving stories out of air you've never breathed.

Odette did not ask to know more of what happened to me, and I did not want to tell it. But she understood the pain.

Maybe she's right. Maybe war was just the backdrop, the setting against which we tried to make a normal life. Those of us who were young, who came from troubled places: for us famine was normal, then war and servitude. The death and mutilation we witnessed. Go where you are sent, take what you are given. Don't talk or question. Don't try to think.

I don't know anything else. How do I separate cruelty from war? How can I be other than this woman, hiding the girl who is always frightened and hungry? I feel the kindness. I don't know how to accept it.

At least now I've tasted champagne. The bubbles are a little like the kvass Auntie Safronia made from black bread crusts and a handful of raisins. Murky peasant brew that quenches thirst on a hot summer day better than spring water, better than tea, while the yeasty tang cools your mouth with sweet effervescence, a taste of earth and home.

Champagne is not like that. Not at all.

38

She doesn't wear the hat, not for a long time. Past her birthday and well into winter, it occupies its place on the hatbox like a museum exhibit meant to be admired but not touched. Her room is so small, every detail is clearly visible from all angles; the hat proclaims its presence even in the dark. Marfa does not need to raise her head from the pillow to make out its shape in the ambient light from the night sky.

It pleases her to know the hat is there. She thinks of it while she's working in the café, or half-listening to Meti read out loud in the evening, or hanging his bed sheet to dry over two chairs near the kitchen stove. She is too modest to use the clothesline in the courtyard, even though all the tenants recognize her and seem indifferent to her coming and going. They nod but do not smile; no one talks to her, not even about the weather. Marfa does not find this strange.

Meti knows nothing about the hat. She has not showed it to him, or told him. It wasn't meant to be a secret, but why not? Her life is nothing but secrets—events, emotions, regrets—each unspeakable for its own reason.

When she walked home from Odette's shop, the hat was a nearly weightless but palpable adornment, there, on her head, for all to see. The air was warm, the sun just setting. If anyone thought it incongruous, a working-class woman's affectation, she was too giddy with champagne to notice, too happy in her growing friendship to care.

Sober, at home, she was content to set it aside, to contemplate its elegance another day.

She will wear it, of course she will. When the time is right.

PART 3

1

Fatma grows impatient with the bride and her older sister, who come daily to supervise the food preparations for the wedding. "Our mother is too sick to come herself," the sister says. "This is the last wedding she will see. Everything must be perfect."

When they are gone, Marfa hears Fatma mumble, "Perfect. What is perfect? As if I haven't been cooking since I could reach the stove."

It is to be a large affair, with guests coming from Amsterdam, Frankfurt, Zurich. Fatma does all the cooking herself. Days before the event, she prepares marinades, buys quantities of eggplants, peppers, tomatoes, huge bunches of mint and dill and parsley. She orders extra cinnamon, sumac, cardamom, sunflower oil, black pepper, salt. In the pantry, ropes of spicy beef sausage have hung, drying, for a month or more.

She arrives even earlier each day to make the *pide* bread for the café—a task she still does not trust to Marfa's foreign hands. As the wedding day approaches and the pace of preparation accelerates, she leaves Marfa to cook nearly all the food for the restaurant patrons, though nothing leaves the kitchen without Fatma's taste approval.

Casual conversation in the kitchen has nearly stopped. It's not her first wedding, but there's so much to do. Fatma moves around her space—from chopping table to stove, pantry to wash sink—with seasoned confidence and no wasted time.

Two days before the big day, the halal butcher delivers lamb for roasting and stewing, slabs of beef for grinding and kebabs. The bride and her sister arrive as he is leaving. The sister peppers him with questions. She pokes the meat, examines it for fat, sniffs it for freshness. "And chickens? Where are the chickens?" she demands.

"Tomorrow," he grumbles. "They're still clucking today."

When he is gone, the sister holds out a sack. "Our grandfather sent these pine nuts, from Italy, for the helva. He is too frail to come."

"The helva is ready." Fatma's voice has an icy edge. "I used semolina and sesame. What you ordered."

"How much did you make? Let me see." The sister drops the sack on the table. The silent bride is blushing, either from nervousness or embarrassment at her sister's arrogance.

"Marfa —" Fatma says, but Marfa is already in the pantry. She brings out a tray of the milk-sweet confections, formed into festive shapes: flowers, shells, stars, crescent moons.

The sister surveys the tray, sniffs again. "Yes, all right. But we'll need more. I'll not sacrifice the blessing on my sister's marriage for lack of helva." Before Fatma can speak, she adds, "Our father will pay." She sweeps toward the door, saying over her shoulder, "Use the pine nuts this time."

The bride whispers, "I like sesame." Marfa, risking Fatma's displeasure, gives her a star to taste. "Mmm," the bride says, and follows her sister meekly out the door.

And that is how Fatma ends up with more helva than anyone can use. With time running short, she and Marfa stay late. Marfa boils the milk and sugar while Fatma browns pan after pan of pine nuts and semolina. When Meti turns up at closing time, Marfa shakes her head. Her hands never stop pressing the cooled mass into forms, unmolding the finished ones onto wooden trays. "Not tonight," she says, inclining her head to the wash sink. "See all those dishes?"

In the end, the bride's sister takes only the pine nut helva, leaving Fatma with two hundred sesame confections. Fatma covers the trays with cheesecloth, leaves them at the end of the worktable. "Selim," she says to her brother, "give these away to everyone who comes. Have them wish the bride and groom good health and eternal happiness. Take some home, Marfa. They're paid for."

2

I'm glad Fatma gave me helva treats from the wedding to take home. Now I can repay Odette for her generosity with something special. Makes me feel more like a friend than a supplicant.

Fatma says helva brings good fortune; it's an essential part of weddings and naming ceremonies, a touch of sweetness against a perilous future.

Does it only work if you believe it?

3

Odette sits just inside her workroom, where she can keep an eye on the shop's door while hemming a spring coat the color of lilacs for a customer. She tells Marfa about the Mummers' Parade. "It's on Mardi Gras, next Tuesday. How long have you lived here? Don't tell me you've never seen it."

Marfa has seen it. It was the year after the war ended. She was swept along by exuberant crowds streaming toward the Grand' Place. Her French was too hesitant, inadequate to asking anyone what was going on: a political rally, a demonstration? One woman, seeing her confusion, addressed her in Flemish, with much waving of arms and open-mouthed laughter. Marfa understood nothing, remembers only the word *appelsienen*, and the glint of a gold-capped tooth.

The parade was an odd spectacle: men in flamboyant ceremonial costumes, wearing tall headdresses topped with billowing ostrich plumes, swung openwork baskets from one hand while flinging oranges—*appelsienen*—into the cheering crowd with the other. None of it made any sense. Not the extravagance of the exotic fruit nor the press of happy people so lately struggling with food rationing, many surely still mourning their dead.

She worked at the tavern then, cleaning rooms, serving beer. By the time she freed herself from the crowd, she was late for her shift. No one seemed to care; the spirit of celebration had left even her taciturn employer in a good mood, in spite of the chilly spring weather.

Marfa hadn't liked the jostling crowd. The shoving was too much like the roundups, the transports only recently ended, getting pushed along with others to an unknown destination certain to hold new humiliations. The high spirits of the people around her did little to dispel her dread and sense of suffocation. Since then, she had learned a little about the Mummers and their customs, but had not cared to participate in their parade.

"You are Orthodox, yes? You celebrate Easter." Odette runs her fingers over the hem to smooth out any puckers. She knots the thread, clips it, and lays the work aside.

"Easter? Yes, but not like this. Not with dancing in the streets."

"What do you do for Mardi Gras? What's your tradition?"

Marfa raises her teacup, sips. "*Blini*. Pancakes," she says. "Buckwheat, with sour cream and caviar, when we can get it. Or plain, with honey and stewed fruit."

"Pancakes," Odette repeats. She plucks a star from the box of helva treats Marfa brought from the café for their weekly get-together.

"You make it sound dull. It isn't. We gather with friends, family. Everyone brings something—homemade wine or fruit brandy, vodka, their own preserves or sausage or pickles. *Maslenitsa*, we call it. It's a full week of feasting, before Lent begins."

"When was the last time—" Odette doesn't finish the question, but Marfa understands.

"Back home, just before the Germans came to my village. We had nothing, but made a celebration anyway, everyone adding what they could." She grows quiet.

"And since then?"

"I went to a parish dinner at the Russian church. My friends Galina and Filip were leaving for America in a few days, taking their baby, my goddaughter, with them; I was devastated to see them go. The other people were strangers to me, even though they spoke my language. I haven't gone again."

"You mean to the church, or to the pancake feast?" Odette takes another helva treat. "These are so good," she says, her mouth full. "Nutty and just sweet enough."

Marfa smiles and nods her thanks. "Both," she answers after a pause. "With my only friends gone, I felt adrift. And I'm not religious. Church only makes me think of my auntie and … and other people I've lost."

"Ah, Marfa." Odette gets up and paces the length of the shop. She stops in front of her friend. "Everything for you is tied up with something else. Something sad or lost or painful. Your head is full of reasons not to do things."

Marfa opens her mouth to reply.

"No, don't say anything. I'm not done." Odette takes another turn around the floor. "Look. I know the things that happened to you are bad, and some of them are terrible. I know you miss people you love. But here you are! And there is life all around you." She squats at Marfa's chair, her hand on the armrest. "Take some."

Their eyes meet. Odette's firm gaze holds a question. Marfa is startled by the unexpected attack, the candor in Odette's words.

"All right," Marfa sighs. "I'll come to the parade. If Fatma will let me."

"If! If! Of course she'll let you. It's Mardi Gras. You only have to ask." Odette straightens up.

"Will you come?"

"I have to watch the festivities from the window. Not that anyone will be buying anything, but Madame insists the shop stay open. If you come here, I won't let you in. I want you in the square, catching oranges. Yes?"

Marfa puts her teacup on the edge of the worktable. She takes a helva crescent from the box, breaks a piece off the end. She holds it a moment between her fingers before placing it in her mouth. "Yes." Her tone betrays neither surrender nor anticipation.

Odette fits the lilac coat over the tailor's form. She runs her hands down the slubby linen, removing stray threads and bits of lint. "Good," she says. "And wear your hat."

4

Talking about traditions was difficult. Why am I so detached from my own life? So empty. Everything from the past, as Odette says, is either painful or sad. Everyone is, in one way or another, lost to me.

Petro, dead. Auntie Safronia—how old would she be now? Past ninety. Dead or might as well be. No way back for me across the border, impossible to get news. Galina and Filip and their sweet child, an ocean away. Even the German went back to Düsseldorf, to his wife. Tolik. Is there enough grief in the world to bear my guilt?

Stop, Marfa, think. Is it so bleak?

Meti is good to me. Odette would say, accept it. It's there in front of you, offered with an open hand. Take some. Who is to say what you deserve.

Odette is not afraid to shake me up, to tell me what is true. When she dances with her gendarme, she does not live in the past or worry about the future. Does she?

I will go to the parade. I will wear my hat. Who knows if I will catch any oranges. But I will go. Yes, I will.

5

They rise earlier than usual this day, stop to breakfast on soft buns and café au lait at the corner bakery. The day is seasonally chilly for early March; a clear sky holds the promise of sunlight.

"Fatma said I have to make the soup, marinate the lamb kebabs, and chop many vegetables before I go to the parade." Marfa pinches off a strip of crust and dips it into her cup. "It's nice of her to let me go."

Meti watches her eat as if she were a child on a birthday outing. He insists on walking her home after every night they are together. There's something formal about this gentlemanly impulse. She feels both protected and, lately, a touch belittled by it, and also amused. As if she has not walked alone most of her life, in places much less safe than this working-class part of the city.

"Why is this parade suddenly important to you? I know you hate crowds. It will be insanely packed." He shakes his head. "All those tourists and country folk."

"That's what Fatma said, too. We made extra baklava yesterday because it's what the tourists want." She holds her cup in both hands, raises it to her mouth but does not drink. "I'm never going back to my village, now that the Soviet border is closed to everyone but movie stars and ballet dancers. I can't see ever going to America, either. This is my country now." She finishes the coffee, gets up to go.

"Mine, too," he says. "But I don't have to drink their famous beer or wear wooden shoes, or participate in their Catholic festivals. Still, if it makes you happy..."

"Yes, Meti. It will make me happy. Meet me at the lion fountain at noon. Don't be late."

In her room, Marfa puts on a clean blouse and runs a comb through her hair. She lifts the hat with both hands, centers it on her head. *No, not like that. How did Odette do it?* She shifts it back and tilts it, the feather curved over her ear toward the back of her neck. *Yes.* She pins it in place.

When she passes the landlady on the stairs, she smiles.

The café is nearly full, in spite of the early hour. Tourists occupy most of the tables, drinking coffee, eating baklava. The air vibrates with languages—English, Italian, German—and loud laughter.

Marfa arrives just in time to hear Selim tell a middle-aged woman at the door, "We don't serve unaccompanied women, Madam."

The woman has a souvenir flag tucked into the pocket of her wool blazer, a package from the chocolate shop in her hand. She looks stunned. She gestures at an empty table. "But... but I'm meeting my friend..."

"I'm sorry, Madam." Selim holds the door open, closes it firmly once she has stepped outside.

Marfa walks quickly through to the kitchen, her head down. She is self-conscious, as if she, too, does not belong here, the hat a lead weight against her temple. She wants to tell the woman, go somewhere else. This is no place for you, it's a club for Turkish men. None of these other people should be here.

But why not? There is no indication, no way a passer-by

would know. The café sign says *Ankara*, next to a tea tray drawn in charcoal on a beige placard. Nothing to tell the uninitiated to stay away. *It's so hard to know the rules.* Catering to tourists in a holiday mood, in the spirit of a national celebration, is good business, but there are limits, it would seem. Marfa feels sympathy for the lone traveler, the woman who only wanted breakfast in a Turkish teahouse in Brussels, a souvenir of her time away from home.

In the kitchen, Fatma's glance lingers a moment on Marfa's hat. For the first time since putting it on, Marfa suffers a twinge of doubt, as if the feathered adornment is broadcasting something about her character that is untrue. Or perhaps something she would prefer the world not to know. Caught up in the scene at the door, she had failed to notice any reaction from Selim and the few regulars at their usual tables. Had they followed her with their eyes?

She unpins the hat and lays it on a high shelf, on a stack of clean kitchen towels.

"Start the marinade first," Fatma says. "Make plenty. I ordered extra lamb, for the foreigners." She scores the *pide* dough with a blade, makes indentations along its surface with her fingers. "They like kebabs, the tourists."

"We like kebabs, too," Marfa says. She lets the words slip out without thinking. She catches her breath. *We?* Fatma must think it presumptuous of her to include herself in this exclusive community. She blushes, but Fatma, who is sliding the bread into the oven, does not see.

Time passes quickly. Marfa chops vegetables, remembers to stir the soup, scooping the lentils up from the bottom of the pot, skimming the cloudy foam off the simmering surface. By the time Fatma's fresh-faced thirteen-year-old niece arrives to lend a hand, the worktable is lined with bowls heaped with onions, peppers, tomatoes, squash. Parsley, mint, and dill are ready; their aromas blend with the spiced eggplant Fatma sautees in her largest iron skillet.

Marfa wants to stay. This food, this work, these people— are they not more important to her than some arcane medieval parade? Some religious tradition for which she feels no affinity whatsoever, that she has promised to attend only at Odette's insistence.

Fatma glances at the clock. "Go now, or you will miss everything. The square fills rapidly."

Marfa hesitates, her hands immersed in slippery raw lamb cubes. She holds a partially filled skewer aloft; sweetish pungent marinade drips from her fingers. "I'll just—" she starts to protest.

"We will finish." Fatma hands the skewer to her niece, who takes up the task with cheerful energy. "Go."

Marfa pumps water over her hands once, twice, to remove the sheen of olive oil and spices. When she reaches for a clean towel, she sees the hat. In the frenzy of food preparation, she has forgotten about the hat.

She sweeps it off the shelf, turns to thank Fatma again, but Fatma waves her away. "I'm busy," she says. "Go." In the café's WC, Marfa peers into the pitted mirror, no bigger than a school notebook, which hangs askew from a single nail. She arranges the hat, threads the hatpin through the velvet crown, straightens her blouse and skirt, and leaves.

The narrow streets leading to the Grand' Place are teeming with people. Marfa joins the flow, too preoccupied with worry to object to the press of bodies all around. Will Meti remember the meeting place? Will he come? What will she do if he does not?

At the entrance to the square, she pushes her way to the lion fountain. She stands aside, out of the way of exuberant children who laugh and splash each other and pay no attention to half-hearted adult scolding.

Meti is not there.

6

We like kebabs.

Who, exactly? This little universe, this restaurant and its busy kitchen, where everyone who steps inside leaves a different reality at the door. Myself included. Yes, included, drawn in. Embraced by the warmth, like that time in the snowstorm, the steamed-up windows, the comfort of sweet hot tea.

Without Meti, what would have happened? Me, unaccompanied like that unhappy tourist, a woman outsider best left alone, her motives, her very life viewed with suspicion. I'd like to think the weather would have made a difference, mitigating the harsh rules with a touch of charity, compassion for another's suffering. I'd like to think so.

Or is it we the larger world, we refugees, grateful for work and shelter, unable to erase the memory of hate and arbitrary cruelty.

We, too, like your kebabs.

People, immigrants, who came with hope, bringing a shawl, a book, the words to a song, a precious heirloom. Weaving their thread of history into the new cloth of their adopted country, their children speaking the old language with the accent of strangers.

The tourists and their photographs, who take away with them the taste, the color of a place. Why do so many dismiss them with disdain, while pocketing their eagerly spent money? Are we not all curious to see how other people live?

Kebabs. Kebabs for everyone.

Who am I now? No home for me among the Russians or the Ukrainians and their church-centered outlook. Auntie Safronia believed, deeply; I cannot fake a piety I do not feel. I did not add my voice to the women on the bridge reciting the Lord's Prayer, chanting Gospody pomiluy, *trusting God's mercy to carry them across the merciless river. I was silent. No mercy for me. No mercy for my child.*

It's the food I miss, sometimes. The simple dishes: sauerkraut soup, onion and potato pie, buckwheat blini with sour cream. Would Meti like them? Should I ask?

Here in this crowd I am alone. Where is Meti?

7

Marfa can't say why it's suddenly imperative that Meti come. She is not lost; she knows every corner, every street lamp and awning of this celebrated square. If anyone asked her, she could direct them to the Italian glover, or the shop that sells Bohemian crystal and Murano glass, or Irish table linens. She can tell anyone where to buy chocolate, marzipan, nougat, pralines; where to watch Belgian lacemakers at work on their traditional designs. Leather goods, lingerie, gentlemen's fine shirts—she knows them all, even though she has only admired their wares from the street. Even if the only door open to her is the dress shop where Odette works: a development that still, after all these months, strikes her as bizzare.

No one will ask her anything, except perhaps to step aside so they can get through.

She pushes her way toward the wall near the lion fountain, where she can stand her ground, resist the pull of the shifting throng. She scans the crowd, looking for the one familiar face.

She breathes deeply to quell her anxiety. These people are here for a good time, she reminds herself. It is not a roundup. There are no trucks, no railway cars waiting to take anyone away. No Gestapo. Still, she feels out of place, not at all sure she belongs here among the revelers.

Where is Meti? Was it foolish of her to insist he join her?

The crowd turns toward the sound of music approaching

from a side street. Trumpets, trombones, drums and cymbals, the barrel drone of a tuba. The sweet notes of a clarinet rise and linger above the brass.

Among the tourists in travel clothes, there are women in wide skirts and starched caps, men wearing blouson shirts, tunic vests, breeches tied at the knee with black, red, and yellow ribbons. Children in miniature versions of the national costume dart through the crowd like songbirds released from captivity. The smell of roasted chestnuts, fried potatoes, and beer, overlaid with sweat and exuberance, is stifling, in spite of the cool breeze.

The music grows louder. People pick up the tune; they form impromptu groups and sing in unison, only to break up and join others in random new configurations. Everyone knows the words; even the tourists soon learn the repetitive refrain.

Marfa watches an old couple hold each other by the waist and move together with the ease of long acquaintance. They appear to take pleasure in the dance—a kind of two-step punctuated by rhythmic stomping of their wooden shoes—without speaking or smiling.

The crowd turns toward the approaching band. "Here come the Gilles!" Marfa hears on all sides. People move closer to the designated parade route, press against the barriers. Small children ride on men's shoulders. "The Gilles, the Gilles!" they shout, as the first plumes come into view at the far end of the square.

Marfa feels torn. The enthusiasm has penetrated her reserve; she, too, wants to go closer, with the others, but is reluctant to leave the meeting place. How will Meti find her if she walks away?

And then he is there, cupping her elbow. "Oh, Meti." She leans briefly against his chest, lays her hand on his arm. "You're here."

"I almost didn't recognize you." He eyes her hat. "What's this?"

She touches the velvet edge. "My hat. Do you like it?" Her glance is both coquettish and defiant. "What are Gilles?" she asks, turning back to the spectacle, craning to see above the heads in her way.

"Gilles are mummers. See their masks, the heavy black painted eyebrows and little beards, the red mouth?" He stoops to her, speaking into her ear over the noise. "They represent mimes in whiteface, from medieval times, itinerant performers who went from town to town to entertain the people."

They push forward. Marfa keeps a tight grip on Meti's hand. "How do you know that?"

"I read it in the newspaper, last night."

Through a break in the mass of people, Marfa gets a glimpse of the marching mummers. The masked ones have passed, followed by bare-faced men in identical costumes— loose pants topped with shirts and long vests, all in red, black, and yellow Belgian flag colors. The painted *sabots* on their feet thunder against the cobblestones.

Each carries an openwork basket filled with oranges. She watches them reach in and fling the fruit in a wide arc, one piece at a time, into the crowd. Meti raises his free hand above his head and plucks a flying orange out of the air.

"The hats!" Marfa exclaims. "Look at those plumes. They must be at least a meter high. Do you think they're heavy?"

"You'll have to ask an ostrich," he says. "The one that

gave up its tail feathers for Belgium's glory."

"They're beautiful, so grand, the way they stand tall and move with the wind. And who are those men with the sacks?"

"Those are *Orange Porteurs*. Their job is to keep the baskets filled with oranges."

"You read that in the newspaper, too?" Marfa teases.

"No. I saw them doing it, before I found you. See the bright orange badge they wear? It has their job title on it."

The Gilles are followed by a contingent of men, women, and children in peasant dress, then Harlequins in colorful motley. A band of Pierrots come last, their billowy white costumes, set off by ruffled collars and big black buttons, dazzle the eye in the afternoon sun. When the parade has passed, the musicians gather in the center of the square. They play tune after tune, all with the same rhythmic tempo, good for marching or dancing.

The crowd begins to thin out. The taverns fill up with thirsty patrons; long lines form at fried potato kiosks and ice cream carts. The cobblestones are slippery with smashed fruit and trampled orange peels, the pungent citrus aroma now mixed with the scent of dog droppings and the yeasty tang of beer. Marfa watches a small boy peel his orange and devour it in two greedy bites, swipe the juice off his chin with the flat of his hand.

She wants one, but not the one in Meti's pocket. She wants her own.

Besides, Meti is talking to some men she recognizes from the café. They stand in an impenetrable circle, each with a lit cigarette concealed in the palm of his hand. Why do they always look so serious? It's as if their minds are always filled with sober news or thorny problems.

She scans the ground. There, under the stone lip of the lion fountain's basin, there's one that rolled away from the general mayhem to a place of relative safety. It looks drenched but intact. Marfa keeps her eye on it, as if it will disappear if she turns away. She edges toward the fountain, stoops to pick up the orange. It's not perfect; the peel is cracked along one side, but it will do. She straightens up, wipes grainy street dirt off the fruit, and runs her wet hand down her skirt.

"What are you doing? You can't eat that, it's not clean." Meti is scowling at her, and she is suddenly angry. *Don't tell me what I can eat*, she wants to say. *I'm not your child.* She shrugs, turns away, and finds herself face to face with Odette.

"Look at you, in your new *chapeau*. Now all you need is a good dress," Odette says with laughter in her eyes. "And some shoes."

Marfa is not laughing. Meti takes her arm and starts to guide her away from the fountain. She resists; the orange in her hand feels cool against her skin. "Oh," she says. "Meti. This is my friend Odette."

"*Enchanté.*" He sounds polite, but Marfa catches how his glance takes in Odette's curly tinted hair, her lipsticked mouth and manicured nails, her tailored dress. "Did you enjoy the parade?"

"As parades go, why not. Everybody needs a little diversion." Odette retreats into the crowd with a barely noticeable wave in Marfa's direction.

"Your friend?" Meti asks softly as they walk away. "Since when?"

Marfa does not reply. She peels the orange with

deliberate fingers and eats it, one sweet wedge at a time.

8

Oranges. They don't grow in this climate. Here the wind sweeps in from the North Sea without warning and leaves a trail of inverted umbrellas, abandoned hats, and cracked flower planters in its wake; it knocks you off your feet and runs off, laughing. It's no place for exotic tender fruit. It's a miracle the daily spring drizzle held off for the parade.

I asked Meti.

Spain, he said.

Spain?

Yes. Sixteenth century, when the low countries were under Spanish rule. Before there was a Belgium. It's complicated—royal marriages, exploration, the New World.

Complicated? More complicated than the history of Ukraine, Galicia, Belarus, Poland? People not knowing from one day to the next which country their village was assigned to, which ruler's portrait to hang on the wall.

So oranges are from Spain. I guess that's why good Dutch and Belgian children get oranges in their sabots on Christmas morning. And the ostrich feathers on the Gilles' heads?

The plumed headdresses, that represents Peru, Spain's conquest of the Incas.

Did you read that in the newspaper too?

No. Serge learned it in school.

Ah. Serge.

But why mummers, then? And why have it on Mardi Gras?

What's the connection?

I don't know, woman. Too many questions. It's traditional, that's all. You must have some odd customs for which no one remembers the reason.

That got me thinking. I don't know, but maybe it happens in families, too. How Auntie Safronia always folded her pillowcases the same way—two lengthwise folds, then in thirds, crosswise. She would do them over if I did it wrong. Without a word, she would unfold and refold them to her satisfaction. When I asked, she said, That's the way my mother did it, and her mother before.

Sometimes it's foolish to go looking for a reason for things.

I like the hat, he said.

And the feather?

The feather looks good, with your hair. But eating the orange, that was stupid. Who knows what you might have picked up off the street. People have died from less. I thought you had better sense.

It takes more than a little street dirt to finish me, Meti. I have enough sense to know that.

What made him so ardent, after, waking me at dawn for more, urgent, insatiable? The green feather or the tainted fruit?

How did Odette understand I needed this hat, this feather? By instinct, or experience? It had to be green and curve like that past my ear, along my neck.

I never told her about Meti. What would I say? I'm with this man, don't ask me why.

She looked at him as if she knows everything. No need for questions.

Nobody knows everything.

Meti says Serge is back.

9

His footsteps on the stairs are bold and loud. Marfa has barely enough time to duck into the bedroom before he bursts through the door. "Papa," he says, his face radiant. "I have great news."

"For all the neighbors?" Meti drapes his newspaper over Marfa's coffee cup. "Close the door, Serge."

"It's a student art show. They've taken two of my pieces." Serge stops pacing the small kitchen from corner to corner and holds up two fingers. "Two."

"In Liège? At the school?"

"No, Papa. Here in Brussels, at a new gallery, next month."

Meti hands his son the water pitcher. "Go down the hall and fill this. You can tell me about it over fresh coffee."

When Serge goes out, Meti enters the bedroom. "You might as well join us, Marfa."

Marfa sits on the edge of the bed. She looks frightened, pale. "I don't want him to know."

"Why not? Why the hell not? If we get married, will that have to be a secret, too?" Serge returns with the water. "Get dressed," Meti hisses.

Serge watches his father lift the cookie tin that serves as a coffee container from its place on the windowsill. "Why do you stay in this primitive place?" he gestures at the dry basin, the portable stove, the crockery on a single shelf near the window. "The new buildings downtown have water in every flat, and you don't have to line up with your neighbors to empty your chamber pot. *Maman* says —"

Marfa hears Meti fill the kettle and put it on to boil. "Yes," he says. "At three, four times the rent. And the street noise, from the boulevard. Living with your windows shut and the door locked." He taps the spoon against the edge of the coffee pot with a harsh ring that sends a shudder up Marfa's spine. "You think you have all the answers."

"Ah, Papa. Let's not argue. Live where you like." The chair Serge pulls out from the table scrapes against the linoleum. "Is this your last cigarette?"

"Since when do you smoke?"

"Everyone smokes at school. Even the girls." Serge strikes a match and holds it a moment before lighting up. "You must have more. You always do."

"Somewhere," Meti mumbles. He checks his pockets, comes up empty. "Go get me a fresh pack."

Serge stirs sugar into his coffee. "Am I your errand boy? You'll need more in fifteen minutes, anyway. Go yourself." His laugh has an edge to it, as if he's unsure his impertinence may not have crossed a line between them. "Then I'll tell you about the show."

Meti sighs and leaves. His receding tread is heavy on the stairs when Serge glances up to see an unopened pack of cigarettes on the corner of the bedroom dresser. "Papa, wait," he calls out and steps into the room, but the street door is just closing.

He turns back toward the kitchen, the pack of Murads in his hand, when his eye registers a movement in the dim recess of the room. One glance takes it all in: the nightgown she's wearing, the bare feet, the dress on a hook in the wall near the bed. Her averted eyes, the hand at her parted lips, thumbnail between her teeth.

Marfa looks up, presses her hands into her lap. "Serge," she says. "Hello."

10

I suppose I expected it would happen one day. Not like that, though, not sitting on the bed in my nightgown. Hiding.

I was not ashamed.

His face going white then deep red and white again. I knew there was someone, he said. But you ... why... how long...

Tell me about the show.

The show? You want to hear about the show? Now?

Yes. Tell me about the show.

Marfa, how can you, how can I...

Tell me.

And I meant it. I had nothing to say; he might as well do the talking.

Well. Remember the bee? The day we stayed in the studio, and stomped on the paper, and you asked for the bee?

Of course I remembered. Those minutes that felt like stepping into a sunlit meadow after coming out of a cold dark forest, or letting river water stream off my clothes. Away from fear and death. If only for a moment, until the fog of guilt descended again, wrapped me head, shoulders, heart in unforgiving memory. I remembered.

So I used that technique, painting on rug canvas, with silk underneath.

A bee?

No. I made shapes, overlapping swirls in bright colors, kaleidoscopic patterns.

He waved his arms through the air so I could almost see what he was describing.

Meti stood in the bedroom doorway, two packs of cigarettes in one hand, a paper cone in the other. Neither of us had heard him come in. He set the things down on the dresser, flung the flowered shawl over my shoulders. Too late for modesty!

I bought breakfast buns, he said, from the bakery.

And we ate them, with jam.

If we get married, Meti said. The words echo in my head like the simple tune of a popular song playing on the radio. They didn't fully register until much later, me here in my room, the bee picture on the wall.

11

They meet by chance a few days later, at the grocer. She is waiting her turn at the counter, reaching for her change purse, when she spots Serge approaching from the baked goods section.

"Marfa. You shop so late?" He looks genuinely pleased to see her.

"After work," she nods. "Do you live nearby? I thought—"

"No. I'm near the Gare du Nord, but the shop in my neighborhood doesn't sell these." He grins and holds up a packet of waffled vanilla biscuits. "I simply must have one or two before bed. Loved them since I was small. I guess *Maman* let the supply run out while I was away."

"You should buy two," Marfa says. "If they're so hard to find." She pays, drops her own purchases into her net bag.

"You're right." Serge heads back to the biscuit shelf. "Wait for me," he calls over his shoulder.

They stand on the sidewalk outside the shop in momentary indecision. The evening sky is pale with northern summer light. Serge slips the biscuit packets into his coat pocket. "Do you have somewhere to go? We could have tea." He steps aside to let an elderly couple stroll through, and doesn't see her blush.

"I'm just going home," she says, "but I smell of vinegar and rosemary. And look—" she holds up her arm. "I managed to dip my sleeve in the sauce."

They laugh. "Come." He leads her across the street to the French café. "We'll sit in the corner, where it's darker. No one will notice."

Serge does most of the talking, about Liège and art school, and some gossip from the rug studio. The men in cloth caps went to Morocco for a family funeral and have not returned. Safya's oldest daughter is to be married next year. Chantal's father has died of tuberculosis.

"I did know that, about Chantal," Marfa says. "Meti—" she falters, her voice catches in her throat. "Your father told me."

This time it's Serge who blushes. He orders a slice of plum tart, more tea. Marfa watches him cut the pastry in half. He wields the knife with precise concentration, avoids her eyes. They eat slowly, savoring the freshness of early summer fruit. Neither speaks until the tart is gone.

"Somebody told me about a dream she had, how she slipped off a bridge into the river and her baby drowned," Serge says after a while. He picks at the crumbs left on the plate.

Marfa's spoon scrapes against the bottom of her cup. Her hand trembles. She floats a lemon sliver in her tea. "Who? Who told you that?"

"A girl I met in Liège. A very pretty German girl, a waitress. We were walking in the park. She was upset. It seemed so real, she said. The water, the wind, the people who pulled her out but couldn't save her baby."

Marfa stares at an old man reading a book at the next table, until he notices and shifts his chair out of her line of vision. "Why are you telling me this?" Her voice is a hoarse whisper.

"I don't know, I just thought of it. Maybe those pictures reminded me." He looks up at the décor above the sales counter: Saint Nicholas in his bishop's robe and mitre, and a row of pensive cherub cutouts, their curly heads outlined against fledgling wings. "Funny thing is, she didn't have a baby, not that I know. Maybe she wanted one."

Marfa forces herself to appear calm.

He doesn't remember.

"What did you do?"

Serge shrugs. "I kissed her. She was a very pretty girl." He runs a hand through his hair. "I don't know what to do when women get upset. I get... disoriented. Uncomfortable" He looks sheepish, touches her hand lightly with his fingers. "You weren't upset the other morning, at Papa's. I like that about you, how steady you are."

Marfa flinches and pulls her hand away. "I have to go, Serge. Thank you for the tea."

She is on her feet and out the door, half a block away when she hears him running, calling her name.

Her heart stops. She turns to him.

He is out of breath, his lips parted in an awkward smile. "Here," he says. "You forgot your shopping." He holds out her net bag. Two apples, a tin of sardines, a wedge of cheese, a small chocolate bar.

12

My shopping. And you, Serge, what did you forget? My confession, the words I entrusted to you with such trepidation. To you and to no one else, in these last ten—no, eleven—years, while the murderous river flows and flows.

I'm wrong. It's not the words, or the pain in them, you forgot. It's me. You forgot me.

There are many parks, many walks, many girls. But how can you not remember? That was me, my tragedy. After eleven years, six months, I've told no one but you.

If only it had been a dream.

The other one, the poor thing in the woods back home, before war, before servitude. A blue, slippery thing. No name. Blood on my skirt. Did it have spirit, a heart? No, no.

But Tolik—he had a heart and spirit. He had a voice. He called me Mama. And I lost him. I failed to guard my baby's life. I let the river grope the knot in my mother's shawl and take him. The women who pulled at my coat, dragged me onto the riverbank—they should have let me die.

Do you know how much courage it took to expose my secret agony to you? For what? What part of my ordeal did I want you to understand? What did I expect from you, a boy who feels uncomfortable with women's tears?

You kissed a pretty German waitress while walking in the park, in Liège. To comfort her, you said. Would she take comfort in that kiss if she knew you hardly heard whatever painful thing she confided to you? Because it wasn't about losing a child in the river. Have you betrayed her trust, too?

Many months have passed since we last saw each other. I have to believe your confusion of the two events is a cruel trick of memory. I sometimes forget how innocent you are. How sweet to learn you can't sleep without your favorite bedtime biscuit.

I know one thing. No one will call me Mama ever again. No one.

13

"Meti's a good man." Odette is arranging a new line of summer cotton dresses on the rack near the door. "He's steady," she adds.

Marfa flinches at the word, but Odette, with her back turned to the room, doesn't see. Marfa hears Fatma saying the same words—a good man—but Fatma and Meti share a cultural bond, and many years' acquaintance. "You know that from an introduction on a crowded street, a handshake?"

"It's his eyes. Intense but gentle, too" Odette steps back to inspect her work. "Look at these colors. Rose, forget-me-not, geranium, hyacinth. More like a flower cart than a dress shop."

"I like them. They look cool and pretty."

"They are. But nothing like the kind of couture our ladies are used to. It's as if Madame's new young assistant took over while Madame was napping." She cinches a white belt around the waist of the rose dress, adds a butterfly pin to the collar.

Marfa fingers a gauzy sleeve. "Is that so bad? Maybe they'd like something different. Something new —"

"He loves you," Odette says over her shoulder, her voice flat.

"How do you know?"

"I know."

Marfa stares out at the plaza. Among the tourists, she spots a few habitual walkers: the elderly woman and her dog, the man who comes to feed the pigeons in all weather, the young couple and their new baby. She lays her hand against the glass door. "Maybe that's not enough, to be loved. Maybe I need more. Or less. Yes, less. Without responsibility for another person's happiness." She lifts her hand away and wipes at the imprint on the glass with her handkerchief.

"What, you'd rather be alone, hidden in your room or some restaurant kitchen, drowning in tragic memories?" Odette removes the butterfly pin. She holds up two pendants for Marfa's opinion, holding first one then the other against the neckline of the dress.

"The pearl one," Marfa says. "The teardrop."

14

Steady. That word again. What does it mean? Is it the same for everyone?

Serge said it about me, and Odette about Meti.

I suppose a man who is steady is reliable, doesn't waver in his affections or change his opinions. A good provider. A rock.

But a woman? Is it enough if she can be counted on to keep a household running, to do her work? Cause no trouble.

The incident at Meti's, me sitting quiet on the bed, not making a scene. What else could I do? I've had enough of scenes to make me shut my mouth and let things happen. As things will.

Did that seem steady?

I know Meti loves me, but he wants more than I have to give. What he's asking—it's impossible. What looks steady in me on the outside is smothered trepidation and fear within. Not steady, no. Numb.

Odette has an instinct for reading people, an intuition she needs in her profession. In her world, few things are more personal than wearing the right clothes. She excels in understanding what women want.

But how did she know everything about Meti and me, from a moment's meeting, a casual handshake? Is that instinctive, too? In her own life, she doesn't stumble from one thing to the next, like me. She chooses. I hope her gendarme is as good a man as she deserves.

15

"We should eat here, Marfa." Meti nods toward a row of benches outside the train station.

"Here? It's practically in the street. Can't we picnic in the park, near the monument?"

"I don't think it's allowed, in the park. You know how careless people can be with their half-eaten sandwiches and discarded fruit peels. And the town is full of cafés happy to sell mineral water at twice the price."

Marfa chooses a bench away from the Waterloo station's open doors, where they can enjoy the warm breeze without being on full display to the busy thoroughfare. "This makes me feel like such an immigrant," she says with a pained smile. "Eating on the run." She unpacks the food onto a napkin between them: hard boiled eggs, cucumbers, tomatoes, sliced Gruyere cheese and a baguette.

Meti breaks off a piece of bread and holds it in his hand. A small flock of pigeons takes notice. They crowd around, bobbing their iridescent heads and pecking at the ground, ready to take part in the picnic. "Do you mind being an immigrant? What does it mean to you?" He shuffles his feet to shoo the birds away. "I'm an immigrant too, you know."

She doesn't answer at once, busies herself peeling one egg then another; her fingers move slowly over the slippery surface to remove every bit of shell. "It means —" She sighs, tosses the crushed eggshells to the waiting birds. "You've been here since you were small. Do you feel like an outsider? It's the only country you know."

"I grew up among people determined to keep the old ways, speak the home language. They never let me forget where I came from, the history of that Ottoman place, the conflict that made it necessary for them to leave."

He plucks the soft middle out of his bread and nestles the egg in the hollow. Marfa smiles. "You've probably been doing that since you were little."

Meti nods, smiles back. He devours the egg and bread in two bites. "My mother thought it was uncouth, something I picked up from my Belgian friends. But I did it anyway."

Marfa halves a cucumber, lengthwise. She sprinkles salt on one side and rubs the cut edges together. "I suppose technically I'm still a refugee. As long as I have the Nansen passport, I remain officially stateless. I don't know that it matters. I have work papers, a residence permit, and get medical care at the clinic if I need it. What difference would citizenship make?" She takes a slice of cheese, eats it.

"It makes all the difference, woman! Your papers and permits can be revoked. A change in policy or another international conflict, and you're on your way back to Ukraine, however unjust or illegal that may be. Then what will I do?"

Their eyes meet. The cucumber half she offers him quivers in midair. "Oh, Meti," she says, and looks away.

They take turns sipping cool sweet tea from the thermos cup. When they have eaten everything but the heel of the baguette, Meti starts to break it apart to feed the circling pigeons. Marfa stops him. Without a word, she tucks the bread into her handbag. They buy a paper cone of sour cherries from a roadside fruit vendor and join the stream of visitors making their way to the foot of the Waterloo monument.

Marfa only half listens to Meti's recital of the historical significance of the celebrated Lion's Mound. She doesn't find the man-made grass-covered structure particularly appealing. While Meti drones on about the British, Dutch, and Austrian alliance that thwarted Napoleon's rise toward world domination, she wonders how the thing was constructed. "Meti," she says. "How did they build it, a hundred years ago? And the lion statue on top, how did they get it up there?"

He frowns at the interruption. "I don't know. With ramps and pulleys, I guess. Like the pyramids. Anyway, they claim it stands on the very spot where William of Orange fell, struck down by the French. 1815."

"I know." She points to the plaque outside the gates through which they have just passed. "It says so right there. It also says people in poor health shouldn't try to get to the top. Can you manage it, with your leg? It's two hundred and twenty-six steps."

"My leg is fine," he growls. "Keep moving."

They join the line snaking up the steep staircase to the top of the monument, keeping to the right to make room for the flow of descending visitors.

"You should marry me, even if you don't love me yet." They're standing under the lion's head; the beast's massive paw rests on a globe high above their heads. The globe of peace, Meti tells her.

"You have a wife."

"No, I don't. We... well, we never married. Some misunderstanding about the day, the hour we were to meet at the marriage bureau. Then Serge came, and the war. We settled in, one day after another. Didn't get around to it."

He walks to the guard rail, grasps it with both hands and stands looking at the bucolic landscape, his back stiff. When Marfa joins him he says, without looking at her, "I told her, you won't get my army pension if we don't make it official. She didn't care. Just don't get killed, she said." He makes a quarter turn, sweeps his gaze over the farms and outlying villages that have reclaimed the historic battlefield. "She's a free spirit, nothing practical about her."

"Is that why she paid for art school for Serge, even though you were opposed to it?"

"Yes. It's also why I can't live with her."

"But you love her."

"I love you."

They move toward the stairs, propelled by the pressing crowd eager to move on to the next item on their itinerary. Behind her, Meti rests a hand on Marfa's shoulder and keeps it there until they reach the ground.

16

Napoleon. What can you tell me about Napoleon? Didn't we show him the door, years before Waterloo, before your Wellington or your precious William of Orange? We gave him the ashes of Moscow, the skeletal remains of our own capital burnt to the ground in defiance of his imperial arrogance.

Just because I'm not educated doesn't mean I don't know anything.

I know that Russia has been brutal with Ukraine; the wounds are deep and may be beyond healing. They plundered our wealth, suppressed our language, starved our people.

Who are these Russians? Every Soviet third-grader knows they took government from the Vikings, religion from the Greeks.

And then? Four hundred years under Mongol rule left more than the legacy of splendid Cossack horsemanship; it left a tolerance for tyranny, throwing off one master only to yield to the demands of another. A history of contradictions: Peter the Great's German villages and the gleeful persecution of the shtetl Jews. Byzantine opulence and the abject superstition of the poor. Glittering royalty modeled on the ruling houses of Europe; dynasties built on the backs of serfs and their thankless labor.

You see, Auntie, I did pay attention in school, even if I didn't like it.

Russia is a country that can't decide if its paragon of beauty is the flaxen-haired maiden from the north or the dark one whose eyes and cheekbones reflect her Mongol heritage.

Is our fairytale Ivan a simpleton who hides his wits behind the illusion of shiftlessness, or is he truly lazy, with nothing to gain by working for his callous masters? Until the reward— stepping into the realm of power over his oppressors, marrying the tsarevna—becomes too desirable to ignore. No fool he, our Ivan.

17

Odette is sorting buttons. She scoops a handful out of the basket at her feet and distributes them among several white cardboard boxes in front of her on the worktable. "Size," she says. "The most important thing about a button is its size. Would you believe it?"

Marfa looks on, not eager to help her friend with this task. The buttons look bewildering in their variety: every shape, texture, style, and size. She is not sure she would know how to separate them. She works instead on a skirt she brought from home, fixing the loose hem with quick small stitches, taking advantage of the shop's selection of matching color thread.

"Yes." Odette tosses a few pale tortoise-shell ones, about half the diameter of a *centime*, into a box marked 'shirt.' "And you know who taught me? Madame Régine. This is her basket, her lifetime collection." She pauses. "She made all my mother's gowns."

Marfa looks puzzled. "With buttons on them? For cabaret?"

"No, silly. Of course not. The cabaret gowns were sleek, made to look alluring in the half-lit rathskellers and seedy night clubs where my mother sang. No buttons on them, that you could ever see." She scans the surface of the basket, plucks out four or five large ones in different colors, drops them in the 'coat' box.

"The gowns, do you still have them?"

Odette shakes her head. "When her singing days ended, my mother and I sold them on the street, in the flea market, for rent money. They didn't bring much. During the war years, Madame Régine would use anything she could find—coat linings, or damask tablecloths plundered from a country chateau. Considerably less glamorous in the light of day."

"Who did the plundering?"

"Anyone. When the Germans arrived, in 1940, it was everyone for themselves, you know? Anyway, Madame Régine always said it's all about proportion. The length of the jacket, the width of the sleeve, the cut of the dress, dictates the size of the button to complement the design. Color and shape are important, but size comes first."

"Is this Madame—" Marfa gestures around the shop at the dresses on racks along the walls and on mannequins in the vitrine facing the square.

Odette laughs. "Oh, no. Madame, my employer, knows how to dress today's woman, but she can't sew a straight seam to save her life. Her designs are nothing without the labor of her cousins' hands." She glances around the room at the thread cones, pincushions, tape measures, scissors, and other tools of her trade. "And mine. No, Madame Régine was an artist with the needle. A magician who made beautiful clothing appear under her hands out of nothing anyone would find valuable."

Marfa, her mending done, tucks the folded skirt into her satchel. She picks up a pair of domed shank buttons shaped like swirled chocolate bonbons. She weighs them in her hand before placing them, after a tentative glance at her friend, into the box with other fancy closures. "You said *was*. Is she still alive?"

Odette nods, whether at the sorting effort or the question, Marfa doesn't know. "She's alive, if you can call it living, her joints twisted with rheumatism. Her couture days are far behind her now." She runs her hand idly through the basket; buttons slip between her fingers and spill, clicking and rushing like water down a drainpipe in a storm. "It's closing time. Let's go to Lucien's for a cup of tea."

Lucien's is deserted when they arrive. They buy buttery yeast buns at the bakery counter and order a pot of herbal tea. Odette leads the way to a small round table near the back. She tells Marfa what happened to Madame Régine. How her husband returned from the war with a head wound and suffered a nervous affliction that has progressed through the years until his hands shake so much, he can no longer button his shirt or cut the meat on his plate or lift a spoon to his mouth.

And now his wife, who has cared for him with the help of a weekly visit from a health service nurse, has fractured her shoulder. "She fell out of bed, rushing to answer his call from the toilet," Odette says, her mouth a grim straight line. "And the elderly neighbor who looked in on them every morning has died."

Marfa stirs sugar into her tea. She tries to look sympathetic, but she is not sure why Odette is telling her this story. "Can they live in an old folks' home, where people will take care of them?"

Odette lights a cigarette and blows smoke toward the ceiling. "Have you seen those old folks' homes?" she snorts. "Have you smelled the stink of laundry soap and decay, seen the weariness in the attendants' eyes?" She rips her bun into pieces but does not eat it. "Those are places to go to die, not to live."

In a voice quavering with suppressed tears, she talks about growing up, about the seamstress who spent more time with her than her mother did. How this woman, a stranger, opened her home to a lonely child, nursed her through measles and whooping cough, fed her in the lean years out of her own rations. She taught her how to carry herself, how to survive in a world of men without getting abused. "And she taught me how to sew, so I would always have work."

"Like a grandmother. Like my Auntie Safronia," Marfa says.

"I suppose there are different kinds of grandmothers. I wouldn't know." Odette drops a piece of bread in her tea and fishes it out with her spoon. "She certainly wasn't the hugging sort. Her love revealed itself in dignity, in sensible care I have never experienced from anyone else. And Monsieur. He would read to me—adventure stories and mysteries, Jules Verne, Sherlock Holmes, Dumas, until his hands shook too much to hold a book. He showed me by his example what a good man is, nothing like the ones my mother brought home from the cabaret. The ones who smelled of booze and cheap cologne, whose cool gaze made you feel like a plucked chicken in the butcher's case."

She puts the spoon down on her saucer without eating the bread. "And now my friends need help. More help than I can give them on my Sunday visits."

A young couple comes in, she in dress pumps and a coat the color of ripe plums, he with an aviator scarf draped dramatically around his neck and over the shoulders of his gray suit. Marfa and Odette sip their tea in silence while the two deliberate over the pastry selections. Raspberry cream torte or chocolate Charlotte?

Marfa glances at her friend, notes her clenched jaw, her tense posture, the way her foot twitches of its own accord. She takes a surreptitious bite of her bun, as if enjoying food in this fraught moment is somehow inappropriate, a cause for guilt.

The couple settle on raspberry torte and go on their way, leaving a trail of flirtatious laughter.

"Marfa," Odette says. She leans over the table, her shoulders hunched. "You are the most gentle person I know. Have ever known. And the most capable." She uncrosses her legs, runs a hand through her hair. "These people, these old sick people I love, they need someone to stay in their home, to look after them. At least until Madame Régine's shoulder heals. It breaks my heart that I cannot do it myself. But I must work, and they live in the country, in a village south of Charleroi." She looks away. "And... and I just can't. Maybe it's a defect in my character, a vestige of the selfishness I absorbed from my mother. Maybe I just can't stand to witness their frailty, to watch them sink into helplessness. But I can't. You understand?"

Marfa takes a breath, holds it, exhales.

"We've talked about it, in general terms. They can pay a little, from Monsieur's veteran's pension and their state allowance for the elderly. You would get meals and a room, of course." Odette closes her eyes. She looks tired, her face pale, her mouth sad.

Marfa studies the fleur-de-lis design on the ceramic

teapot. She pours the last of the tea into their cups, rotates her cup slowly on its saucer. The tea's surface shimmers and releases a flowery aroma into the air. "Would they have me, a stranger?"

Odette opens her eyes. "They have no one. I have no one else to ask."

The women drink their tea.

Marfa says. "I will tell Fatma at the café tomorrow. Her oldest will finish school in the spring, she can help out until a new cook is found. So yes, Odette. I will go."

Odette reaches across the table and squeezes Marfa's hands. "Thank you, my friend." She sits back, picks up a piece of her bun and eats it. "And Meti?"

"I will talk to Meti. Which train do I take to Charleroi?"

18

Don't I have to do some penance to earn my place in the world? It's not enough to stumble around or sit and wait to be recognized. Is it? Maybe looking after these old people is a repayment of my debt for being alive. A reckoning.

I never imagined that carefree, sophisticated Odette carries her own burden, a memory of neglect set against a debt of gratitude she cannot repay.

I picture her, a pretty child with clear brown eyes and unruly hair, watching her mother dress for an evening's work. Then alone, touching the things on her mother's dressing table: the curling iron, the rouge, nail polish, eyebrow pencil, lipstick. I see her slip her slim feet into high-heeled shoes, step behind the flowered curtain and stroke the gowns on their wooden hangers. Gowns she loves for their mystery and elegance, hates for the way they force her to be alone most nights. Can she imagine the cabaret world built on fantasy and desire? Can she hear the piano, the horn, the violin, the laughter?

Maybe there's more. Maybe she, too, has hidden places too painful to revisit. Are we all damaged, we women? Yours is not the only trouble in the world, Marfa.

I don't think I've laughed since before Petro went off to war. Oh yes, that one time with Serge, stomping on the paper, the dried paint splatters crackling under our feet. A lifetime ago.

I was a fool to love Serge, to believe he could care for me. And I did love him, I loved him for a delirious forgetful moment.

Look in the mirror, Marfa. See who you are.

Unlike Odette I don't mind solitude. I like it. No questions, no explanations. No empty talk. Haven't I always been an outcast?

Odette can't stand to be alone. I see it in the way she talks to the women who come for a fitting or drop in on a whim to buy something. The way she has them tell her about their mothers, children, lovers—before they're fully aware of treading on intimate ground. I suppose they find her safe, like a hairdresser or manicurist who will keep their secrets as part of her professional services.

She has not asked much about my life, my secrets. Is it because, unlike the women who come and go, their confessions forgotten as soon as they step out of the shop, she considers me a friend? How many times she said to me: no, don't tell me. Because friendship carries obligation—the thing she cannot face?

What I told her that rainy evening in the street was just enough to explain the shawl—but then that's everything, isn't it. The shawl that is my mother, who would have loved me, and my auntie, who did. It stands for my obstinate stupidity and the betrayal of my trusting child.

Galina was my friend during the war, but we didn't need to tell each other anything; we lived it together. I never learned how to confide, how to talk about the stone on my heart.

Look what happened when I told Serge. Never again.

Yet we are alike, too, Odette and I. Our lives have unfolded, giving us what we each need to survive. Her Madame Régine, my Auntie Safronia. She learning the sewing trade, me cooking and housekeeping. We each got exactly what we required from a wise woman who cared deeply about our future.

So I will go. I will help my friend, do this necessary thing,
repay in this small way the life-saving gifts we each received.
She was good to me when she brought me in out of the rain,
offered me cocoa, talked to me, insisted I try on the hat.

She said, when it's your turn to give, you'll know.
Will this close the circle? Will it give me peace?

19

"How long?" Meti sits on the edge of the bed. He reaches for the shirt draped across the painted wooden chair, turns his head sideways. "How long will you be gone?"

"As long as I'm needed, if it works out." Marfa meets his gaze, then looks away. "If we all get along, and they like my cooking." She stares at the lamp on the bedside table, notes the dust ring around the edge of the fluted paper shade. "They're old and sick. Anything can happen."

He puts the shirt aside and lies back down, shielding his eyes with his arm. "Who wouldn't like your cooking," he says. Street noise drifts through the open window: the clang of the trolley, two streets away; a gendarme's whistle; two men's voices in a heated argument about money. The life outside accentuates the long silence in the room. "Why?" Meti says at last. "Why you?"

"Because they need help. Odette says—"

"Odette. I should have known she'd be behind this. Who are they, her relatives? Can't she look after them herself?"

"No. They cared for her, years ago, and now—well, she can't leave the city for more than a day or two, and they need looking after. Daily, not just the occasional visit."

Meti puts his arm down and turns on his side, facing her. "Why?" he asks again. "Why can't you let me take care of you? These jobs, this... this need you have to be busy with something all the time. I can give you whatever you want.

More windows, trees, rose bushes, a cat? We can move out of center city, find a little house with a garden. Stay with me, Marfa."

He lays his hand on her cheek. Marfa closes her eyes, buries her head against his chest.

"I can't explain. You're so good to me. Better—" she lets out a shuddering sigh "– better than I deserve." Meti starts to reply, but she shakes her head. "No. You don't know. I'm not worthy. And I'm not leaving you, not really. I just have to work. I have always worked. Since I was little, Auntie Safronia and I worked all day long, taking care of the animals, the farm, cooking, washing, mending..." her voice trails off, ends in another sigh.

"Marry me. We could have a child. That would be work enough for you, wouldn't it?"

She shakes her head again. Meti feels the heat of her tears on his skin. "What happened to you, Marfa? Who hurt you? Tell me."

"No one. I did it. It was all my fault."

"Tell me."

"I can't," she whispers. "Don't ask me. Let me go."

20

A child. We cannot have a child, Meti. I am not to be trusted with the life of a child.

He is so accepting. How would he change toward me if he knew my unforgivable failing? What if I told him and he turned cold, cut me out of his life? It would serve me right.

Or if he said, It's all right, Marfa. It wasn't your fault. Let it go.

That would be unbearable.

It's my burden. I carry it.

Ask me again, Meti, if I want a house, rose bushes, a cat. Ask me later.

But now I must go. And I will think about you.

21

Marfa has to ask the landlady for a broom to help retrieve her suitcase from under the bed. The bed is narrow, but somehow the suitcase has become jammed into the far corner, against the wall; it takes some hard prodding to work it loose.

She tries to resist the memories, tries not to think about the way she found it on the side of the road, her friend saying, "Take it, Marfa. Whoever left it here won't be back for it." Because no one willingly leaves everything they own by the side of the road, especially in wartime.

She knew that was true, preferred, then and now, not to imagine how it came to be abandoned. She didn't want to think about what happened to the band of refugees just like themselves who left it behind.

Marfa wipes the dust off the cracked leather surface, where traces of dried mildew still bloom in dark patches; the corners are rubbed through to the cardboard frame underneath. She sits back on her heels and lets the past in. How she opened the suitcase, there on the road. Emptied its contents on the ground and watched her fellow travelers take what they could use. She wanted none of it, even though she could have sold or traded the man's shirt and trousers, the shaving brush, the tin cup, the water flask. How long had it been since their group had left the river?

Not long. Not long enough for her to care about what

she might need to survive, with the war just ended and no plan for any kind of future.

She had taken the suitcase, didn't react when Galina pulled a skirt and blouse out of her own bundle and placed them inside. "For you," her friend said. "You're thinner than I am." The only thing she, Marfa, had was the photograph of Auntie Safronia, which she removed from her dress pocket and slipped under the clothes before snapping the latches shut.

Marfa opens the suitcase. She knows what's inside: the Nansen passport, proving her DP status as a citizen of no country; her Belgian residence permit and working papers. She lays those things aside and picks up the photograph.

It is tattered around the edges, creased from years of traveling hidden in pockets or knotted into a dress hem. Auntie Safronia's face is no longer visible, concealed by a water stain the color of strong tea. Marfa studies the figure in its shapeless dress, the old black sweater draped over its shoulders; she sees the sloping roof of the cottage at the old woman's back, the barren wheat field beyond reduced to burnt stubble by the advancing enemy. She weeps.

When evening falls, she puts the documents back in the suitcase, the photograph on top. She folds her clothes, wraps her extra shoes in a kerchief. She adds her alarm clock, clay teapot, plate, knife, fork. Everything fits, with room enough for her sheet, pillowcase, and nightgown. She drapes her coat over the back of the chair, leaves the suitcase open on the seat to finish packing in the morning. The hatbox with her hat inside is on the floor next to the chair.

The night is moonlit. Marfa opens the window to cool air that still holds the last remnants of the day's sun. She sits on the bed, scans the room for anything she may have over-looked, anything that belongs to her. Her eye lands on the bee picture tacked to the wall; the yellow paint dots glitter in the light of her lamp. She turns off the light, lies down. The black pattern of the bee's wings seems to blend into the dark. She can almost hear Serge laughing.

Marfa crosses the room, pulls the picture off the wall. At the window, her hand is firm, her eyes dry. Her mind is still. She lets the breeze take the bee into the night, watches the paper curl and float away, rise, rise, and fall to the ground like a wounded bird.

22

Odette offered friendship. How did she know I needed cocoa and pastries and a little laughter? She has never asked for anything in return. Now she needs me to take her place in what passes, in these postwar years, for family.

I dreamt of Auntie Safronia last night. Did anyone ease her pain, wash and feed her in her final days so she could reach the end with dignity? Did she die alone or with others, ravaged by hunger and disease, or was she dispatched with a merciful bullet to the head? I will never know; I was not there. In my dream I kissed her hardened, loving hands. Auntie, I kiss them now.

Is it selfish of me to want to care for these old people?

I could have said no. I could have said: Odette, I don't know these people. But I feel drawn to go there—to go away from here—to help, to work. To think, or to refrain from thinking.

Meti calms my mind. I sleep longer and deeper when his arm rests on my shoulder, his leg drapes over my hip, his chest warms my back. Is it enough? Is it love?

If I marry him, my status will change; I will no longer be a non-person. An immigrant, not a refugee.

And what else? What else will change? What price for his offer of security?

Will I stop cringing at the sound of thunder, or conquer the fear of mud and rushing water? Will I ever share with him the living nightmare of my greatest failing? Tell him the reason I will never again wear a shawl. And if, like Serge, he dismisses my tragedy, then I have nothing. A room somewhere, menial work, a suitcase under the bed.

I can't decide if I want anyone to take care of me. Do I even deserve to be loved?

Let go, he says. Let go whatever's worrying you. I'll look after you.

How is that different from these old people, who need help because they're too frail to do anything for themselves? If I accept his offer, admit my own peculiar frailty, am I not just as helpless, unable to decide how I will live? As if all it takes to make my life complete is rosebushes and a cat.

Last night, after our supper and his need for me, the tender urgency of the familiar motions followed by the balm of intimate silence, I had to leave. To pack, I said. No, do not walk me home. It's not dark city streets I'm afraid of.

Take this, he said. This pendant, this moon and stars. It is not precious, but it comes from my heart. Think of me when the crescent moon rises, when it cradles the evening stars within its cupped hand, as I do you.

So much feeling and unexpected poetry; I've never heard him talk like that.

Walking home with tears I couldn't let him see, I almost lost my resolve. Like that first night, I almost let my feet take me back to his door.

I almost stayed.

23

"Why didn't you tell me this is all you have?" Meti stops pacing the railroad platform to nudge her suitcase with his foot. "I would have bought you a new one. So you don't look like an orphan."

Marfa is perched on the edge of the bench just outside the waiting room door. She is wearing her coat in spite of the warm day. "I am an orphan," she says.

Meti strides to the tracks and back again, a string-tied parcel tucked under his arm. He studies her—the straight back, sober expression, her hands folded on her lap. He's about to speak, one hand on the parcel, when Odette arrives, ten minutes before the train's scheduled departure. She's carrying a handsome satchel: a basketweave of brown and yellow cotton with raffia handles. Marfa rises to greet her.

Meti goes back to the tracks and peers into the distance.

"Here," Odette says. "Some things for my friends." The bag holds a box of chocolates, a lightweight lap robe, the shape of other treats concealed in its depths. She reaches under the chocolates for a package of gingerbread honey loaf sprinkled with sugar crystals. "It's Monsieur's favorite evening snack, with lots of butter and a cup of chamomile tea." She smiles. "The bag is for you, for shopping."

They stand in awkward silence for many minutes. Meti avoids looking at the women. He shifts the parcel to his other arm, reaches down to wipe cinders off his shoes.

Odette's glance falls on the hatbox at Marfa's feet. "You should wear your hat, for the journey. It's perfect for train travel."

"Is it?" Marfa's laugh has a nervous tremor. "I'm not having an adventure, you know."

"Aren't you?" Odette looks serious, but her eyes sparkle.

"All right," Marfa says. "Give me the hat."

Meti watches Odette lift the hat out of its box and arrange it on Marfa's curls. "I hope someone like you will care for me when I am old," Odette says. "Someone sweet and reliable and thoughtful. Though maybe not so very quiet." She pins the hat in place and steps back.

Marfa shakes her head. The hat's feather stirs and settles, smooth, along her neck. "You will never be old. Me, I have been old all my life. But I do like a little—" she pauses, searches for the word, "– distraction, you know?"

"Go," Odette says. They kiss on the cheek. One, two.

Meti looks away, as if embarrassed by the intimacy that passes between the women, the palpable bond of their friendship.

Marfa puts Odette's satchel down and extends her hand toward his face. She lets her fingers hover, cups his beard without touching. Her eyes are clear, dry. Unreadable. "Goodbye, Meti," she says. "Thank you."

"I wish—" Meti reaches for her hand, but she has picked up her things and is running to the train.

He stands with Odette, watching the train prepare to pull out of the station. "Marfa—" he calls out. He moves closer, holds out the parcel. "You forgot your shawl."

Marfa turns on the wagon step, suitcase and hatbox in

one hand, Odette's bag in the other. The morning sun glints silver off the pendant around her neck. She shakes her head. "I can't, Meti." When their eyes meet, neither smiles. "Bring it when you come."

"Tell them I'll visit on Sunday," Odette raises her voice over the station noise, the last-minute commotion that comes with a departing train, even though no one runs alongside, no one waves or shouts out of windows to those left behind. It's an ordinary train, an ordinary day.

When it is gone, Odette turns to Meti, lays a light hand on his arm. "We could travel together Sunday, if you like."

Meti looks uncomfortable. "We'll see." He hooks a finger through the string on the rejected parcel. "We'll see. Might be better to let her settle in."

Odette drops her hand to her side. "Maybe so, Meti." They have run out of conversation. "Time to open the shop," she says.

Meti lights a cigarette, follows her with his eyes—the swaying skirt and fitted jacket, the confident step of her black pumps. He notes the little hat, and the way the breeze stirs the hair on her neck and shoulders. Hair like Marfa's, the same color and disarray.

Meti

She is gone.

When the station guard approaches me, I have been pacing the platform for two hours or more, long after her train has probably reached its destination.

"Monsieur," he says. "I must ask you not to leave your butts on the ground." He indicates the sand-filled buckets outside the waiting room door with a Gallic wave of his white-gloved hand. I turn to see a trail of Turkish cigarette ends, with their distinctive cardboard mouthpieces, lining the length of the platform. I apologize and bend to pick one up.

"No need," he stops me. "The sweeper will get them now. But in the future..."

We stand side by side. I feel uneasy in his presence; he studies the tips of his polished shoes. "Are you waiting for someone?" he says at last. His hand rests on the baton at his waist in a gesture I take to be habitual rather than threatening.

"No longer," I admit, still unable to move.

"Ah, oui. The young woman with the hat. Your daughter?"

I find my legs then, turn and walk away. Out of the station, into the busy midday streets: women shopping for dinner, school children crowded around ice cream vendors, men two or three abreast, talking.

When I get to Selim's café, I can't help a glance at the plate-glass window. There I am, a man of middle years, no paunch or stoop, dark hair and beard silvered—not unattractively. Old enough to have a daughter Marfa's age? Perhaps.

What did she see? Did I remind her of her father? She spoke about him only once or twice, without admiration or affection. Is that why she left me behind, going off on her own to do charitable work for strangers? She said, for a while. How long is a while? There's no saying how long old people may linger, with good care.

She may have a change of heart, come back on the next train.

She may not return. Goodbye, she said.

Has she left me?

If so, it's not because I'm old. I am not old. I have more vigor now, more life than I felt in my twenties. Better control, more patience, when it matters. We were of one mind in bed, weren't we? No disappointment there. She wasn't thinking of her father then. Damn it, we were happy!

Thank you, she said, and nothing more. And I am guessing again, trying to dig for meaning in her cryptic words, her half-finished sentences, her exasperating silences. Thank you?

... for giving me work.

... for helping me out of the storm.

... for feeding me.

... for not asking too many questions.

... for loving me.

... for letting me go.

I am no paragon of goodness, I have as many faults as the next man. I tend toward laziness, look for the easy way, and yes, the temper, the temper. I blow up at Serge, his foolishness and curious lack of ambition, but never, never at her. Not even when she bedevils me with her silences.

Why did she go?

If she had stayed with me last night, would I know more than I do now, sitting here stirring my coffee, Fatma's baklava untouched on the plate? If we had been alone this morning at the station, without Odette ...

This is your place, your home, she said that one time, when I asked why she kept her hole of a rented room. These are your things, Meti. Your table, your cups and spoons. Your calendar on the wall. Your sheets. Even the robe I wear when I am here is yours. I'm like a shadow here, passing through, she said. A visitor.

So bring your things, Marfa, I said. I'll help you. She only shook her head, with that haunted look she gets when she stops talking.

That look: downtrodden, but also determined, the way women are in hard times, enduring the humiliation of poverty while finding ways to do what must be done. I've seen it on my mother's face, and on my aunts, and Fatma, in unguarded moments before they get back to the task that gets them through another day. I saw it in Marfa the first day, the way she stood before me in the studio and asked for work, her desperation cloaked in a dignity I don't think I could have mustered in her place. I gave her money and she took it; hunger triumphed over pride. But not for long. She paid me back within the week, the coins left on my desk while I was out.

I think I loved her, if not in that first meeting, then very soon after she started working, her head bent over the canvas as if it was the most important thing in the world to her. Industrious, she was, and is, in everything she does. As if she needs to always prove her worth, to earn her space on earth. Why?

At Waterloo, we wandered among the other groupings—families, couples. I liked it, being seen as if we belonged together.

More intimate than Mardi Gras, with its noisy crowds and air of public celebration. I was angry when she picked up and ate the dirty orange. Was it childish defiance of my authority, or did she simply not care? As if she does not think she deserves clean fruit, but is content with what others leave behind.

Was it Odette's presence that emboldened her? Odette, who is the essence of the feminine conundrum. I feel her sensual appeal, but she is not for me. Too much like Serge's mother, looking for a good time with no thought to the future, though she, Odette, is the smarter of the two. When she touched my arm just now, I glimpsed a sadness in her eyes, replaced almost at once with brazen flirtatiousness.

She has stepped between me and my woman for purely self-ish reasons. How did she convince Marfa to do the thing she will not do herself? Whether she lacks courage or ability, or is squeamish at the prospect of caring for the sick, is beside the point. She could have hired a nurse. Instead, she chose to fracture our life, knowingly and deliberately. She may be Marfa's friend, but she is none of mine.

If I go visit Marfa, it will not be a Sunday excursion with Odette.

Oh, Marfa. You have passion and great stores of goodness. I believe you love me, though you have never said so. What keeps you from being the whole magnificent woman you can be? I see us living together, with a child. Wouldn't you like to have a child?

Something happened to you, something unspeakable. I could help you. Let me help you. We all suffered in the war; we're all wounded, whether we show the scars or not. I want you with me as you are, with your moods and secrets, your dark places, because there's something luminous in you that shines through the murk of your elusive nature.

Marfa. I don't know who you are. I love you.

*Maybe one day you'll tell me why you won't wear the shawl.
I can wait.*

Bring it when you come, you said. When you come.

***

Why this book?

Marfa was created when it became clear to me that Galina, the young protagonist in my earlier novel, *Roads*, needed a friend—someone her own age to talk to and share the travails of her journey—a useful plot device known to any fiction writer.

Roads is the story of a family of refugees from the Soviet Union adrift in Germany, unable to return home, looking for ways to rebuild their lives in a post-World War II world.

As the story develops, Marfa suffers a catastrophic incident which, in the context of the book's structure, is explored from the main characters' point of view, not from hers.

But who is she? Where does she come from? What series of events has led her here? How does she live with this horrific loss, endure the consequences of her actions?

And a new book is born, because I need to know.

Marfa's River is not a sequel. It does not continue the story begun in *Roads* through new developments with the same characters. It is an exploration of one woman's struggle to understand the intersection of the everyday with the universal, the need to navigate her life's moments and relate to the people in them, while haunted by her ever-present secret past. It is a portrait of an introvert turned recluse, a woman who speaks little but thinks a great deal, a reluctant player in the relentless progress of her own life.

Acknowledgments

Many people pitched in along the way to make this book possible – first among these are my editors at Apprentice House Press, Carlos Balazs and Kevin Atticks, who helped me polish the work into a cohesive story. I am grateful to Catherine Cassidy, bookseller extraordinaire, and to Juanita Megaro, for their attentive reading of my work in progress and for their cogent suggestions. I am indebted to authors Mark Budman, Nancy Burke, Eleanor Morse, and N. West Moss for agreeing to take time from their own projects to read the manuscript and contribute their words of endorsement, and to the gifted folks in the Cornwall Writers' Circle, who suffered through the entire process, from conception to early drafts to final revisions, with patience, encouragement, and grace. To Celia Galorenzo, whose ear for story detail contributed the cover art idea, and to Bo G. Eriksson for its evocative execution. Finally, grateful to Frank L. Niccoletti, poet and exceptional teacher, who cut me no slack, probing every scene for plausibility, continuity, clarity, and truth.

I thank you, every one.

About the Author

Marina Antropow Cramer's work has appeared in *Blackbird, Istanbul Literary Review, Wilderness House Literary Review, Bloom Literary Magazine,* and *the other side of hope* literary journal. She has read her work at the Hobart Festival of Women Writers (2022), where she served as a workshop instructor. She is the author of the novels *Roads* (Chicago Review Press), and *Anna Eva Mimi Adam* (RunAmok Books). She lives in New York's Hudson Valley.

Apprentice
House Press
Loyola University Maryland

Apprentice House is the country's only campus-based, student-staffed book publishing company. Directed by professors and industry professionals, it is a nonprofit activity of the Communication Department at Loyola University Maryland.

Using state-of-the-art technology and an experiential learning model of education, Apprentice House publishes books in untraditional ways. This dual responsibility as publishers and educators creates an unprecedented collaborative environment among faculty and students, while teaching tomorrow's editors, designers, and marketers.

Eclectic and provocative, Apprentice House titles intend to entertain as well as spark dialogue on a variety of topics. Financial contributions to sustain the press's work are welcomed. Contributions are tax deductible to the fullest extent allowed by the IRS.
To learn more about Apprentice House books or to obtain submission guidelines, please visit www.apprenticehouse.com.

Apprentice House Press
Communication Department
Loyola University Maryland
4501 N. Charles Street
Baltimore, MD 21210
410-617-5265
info@apprenticehouse.com
www.apprenticehouse.com

CPSIA information can be obtained
at www.ICGtesting.com
Printed in the USA
JSHW010823100423
40048JS00003B/156